THE SUNDOWN STALLION

by
TERRY MAY

ROCK HILL PUBLISHING

FOR CHELSEA AND GRAYSON

CHAPTER 1

HUBBARD Anderson pulled the saddle and blanket off the wall and slung it over his shoulder. He carried it along with the bridle out the rear door of the barn, fenders and stirrups slapping at his hips, smelling horse sweat and leather, his thoughts already putting in order the day of work ahead. The hills in the distance were just now turning blue with rusty spots where Spanish oak took on fall colors. A dry October morning; not much dew on the corral gate as he went inside to saddle the mare.

Empty. A section of rails on the ground, splintered, lying in all directions as if they'd fallen from last night's full moon.

Indians? Couldn't be. That was over and done with. He laid the saddle against the wall of the barn he'd just walked out of and inspected the ground. No footprints, and anyway, Indians wouldn't have done that to the rails. Their way had always been to slip in and out like ghosts, take the horse with cunning and silence.

He saw a drop of blood on one of the rails and a fury of unshod tracks cut deep from weight and effort.

A wild stallion. Had to be.

Sarah was surprised to see her husband again so soon. Dishes from their breakfast were still on the kitchen table, the room holding the scents of fried meat and eggs, coffee, the warm remembrance of their words not settled yet.

"Gone," he said, and hung his hat on the peg beside the door, its brim curled down in front to hold off the hard Texas sun. His bronze hair fell into his eyes and he brushed it back with his hand. "A stallion broke down the corral last night, took her off."

Sarah felt tempted to say something light, but the look on Hub's face stopped her. He wasn't going to smile much today. "I'm sorry, Hub. Can you get her back?"

He was pouring himself another cup of coffee, erect and full-shouldered, no sag of defeat evident. Sarah loved him for that and much more than that. "Well, I plan to," he said, and then, against all her expectations he smiled at her and the smile was in his eyes, too, so it was real. "She's joined up with his manada by now, and he'll keep her there if he can. Might be she'd prefer to run wild for a time. Can't say I'd blame her."

"Are you sure it was a stallion?"

He shrugged, sat down at the table with his cup of coffee. "Yeah. There was some blood where he'd nipped at her to make her go. They'll do that; it's how they keep their harem in line."

"That must be hard on the poor mares."

"Oh, I don't know. I think they kind of expect it—like it, maybe." He watched her with a flat gaze, his smile getting wider.

"Well, don't you go nipping on me, Hub Anderson. Not in the daylight, anyway." The baby began crying in another room.

"I'll get her," Hub said.

"You'll have to put a dry cloth on her." Sarah had bought all the white cotton cloth James Harper had in his store a year ago and spent some of the months until Marie was born, cutting and trimming; a lot of work, but the stack beside the baby girl's crib was reassuring now, worth the effort. Marie never suffered from rash. As Sarah had learned from the Comanches during the years she lived with them, she gathered fresh moss off the trees near the river and always stuffed a handful inside before she pinned her daughter's garment. "Don't forget the moss," louder, so he could hear. Her breasts felt full. Marie would be a hungry girl.

CHAPTER 2

H E'D kept the mare on the move, and not just her—the jenny and line-back gelding that Hub had left grazing the night before were with them, but those two ran willingly. The mare required teeth on her flanks and shoulders, the threat of the stallion's pinned-back ears, the fearful twist of his head, his scream. She had no memory of running free like this and the freedom frightened her as much as the stallion did. For her there had always been boundaries, the touch of a hand, the weight of a rider on her back. She was tiring and soon would have to stop for rest despite the urgings of her captor. They had reached flatter country to the north, a place of gentle rises in the land and a far off horizon, so that whatever moved about was easily seen even at long distances.

She saw the other horses long before she scented them. A herd of mares like herself, standing still with heads lifted, watching. Then she was among them, moving against their bodies, answering their throaty greetings, feeling not as frightened, the stallion as full of energy as though he had not run half the night, circling them now, nudging them closer together, circling again and again, then trotting off a short distance to watch with an owner's pride, his chest swelled with conquest, his mane sweeping the tops of tall grasses.

The stallion was a dun, with black mane and tail and black markings on his legs above ebony hoofs. His chest and withers were scarred with relics of wounds received defending his mares against others like himself. Long, deep scars that caused the hair to grow in at odd angles. He was descended from the Spanish ponies of the conquistadores, fourteen hands high, noble in bearing, selfish to the core, insistent on spreading his seed to every mare he encountered. He could run for days at a time without rest, but man was the only threat he ran from.

Everything else he faced with ears laid back, teeth bared and his life on the line. Much like the Indians who had tried to capture him many times and failed. He left the plains three or four times a year to find new mares, but he always returned. This was his home. He knew every watering place, every clump of grass, every spot of shade. And it had been a long time since he had encountered another rival stallion. The young colts of his own manada matured and challenged him, but he easily defeated them and ran them away to other pastures.

The bloody fights that had once been a daily occurrence were no more, the Indians with their trained ponies and their catch-nooses came no longer. It was all his, the grass, the water, the mares. He raised his head and sniffed the air, curled his lip. Another mare had come into season.

* * *

Hub spent half the day walking over his ranch land looking for the mule and gelding, hoping they hadn't run away as well. He saw herds of deer, saw coyotes, saw his own cattle laid up in the shade. And finally he found the spot where four sets of hoofs had merged and turned north and knew he was afoot for sure. It was cool, anyway. A month ago it was man-killer hot out here. Maybe, if the weather held, he could walk her down. But no, he'd walk himself down, too, that way, and it would take too long—too long away from Sarah and the baby. Maybe he should head for his father-in-law's ranch. Ben Turner would be quick to help.

On the other hand he was closest to the place Charlie Boone had bought two years before, bought and fenced in with barbed wire—the first of its kind in that country. He sat down beside a narrow creek, drank as much water as he could hold and filled the canteen he'd kept after the war, buckled it back on and made up his mind. He walked on toward the Boone spread. He wore the moccasins Sarah had made for him months before, a gift he'd never used until now and felt grateful for today—his high-heeled boots would have ruined him before he'd gone half a mile. A canvas morral hung at his waist, supported by a strap across his shoulders. The bag was heavy now, but would get lighter as time went on. It held some biscuits and coffee beans and a metal pot to boil the coffee in; a bridle, too, and wrapped in a clean cloth a double handful of corn he might need when he found the mare.

He reached Boone's eastern fence in the middle of the after-noon, four strands of wire strung on cedar posts planted every ten feet. Charlie had freighted the wire in from San Antonio on ox-drawn wagons, along with the crew he'd hired to put it up. The crew had labored all the winter past, intending to finish before hot weather set in good, and they made it. The way Hub understood it, Charlie intended to bring in Brahman bulls, or Brimmers, as he called them, to breed to the local stock, upgrading the wild brush cattle with the Brahman blood. To do that, he had to control his stock; keep them in a confined area rather than permitting them to wander all over the country as everybody else, Hub included, was doing. And there was going to be trouble over it. The excuse he'd heard for the resentment was that this had always been open range and there was no point in partitioning it off like that. The real reason was that nobody could figure how an ex-slave got ahold of enough money to not only buy a nice-sized piece of property, but to put a fence around it as well. Didn't seem fair somehow.

Hub wandered down the fence line to the nearest gap, opened it up and went through. A trail that made for easier walking led from this gap to the house a half a mile away.

Charlie kept three coon-hounds, all of them black with tan markings, long ears that hung straight down and voices that could lift you off your feet when they went to baying. Two of them came out of the trees near the house to meet him as he approached, and while they didn't quite reach their loudest before Rosabelle's call shut them down, they were plenty loud. After she yelled, the woman came out on the porch and the dogs dropped their tails and went back in the trees, allowing Hub to proceed unmolested. She recognized him as he got closer.

"You out walking for your constitution?"

"I'm walking 'cause I got no choice."

Her face took on concern. "Somethin' happen to that mare of yours?"

"Well, a mustang stallion stole her last night. My other two, as well. I'm left to my own devices."

"You look tired. Come on in the house." Not many of the local people had seen the house Charlie and his wife had built. If they had, there'd have been even more resentment, because it was a very nice house built of fired brick hauled from somewhere north, put up by skilled German masons from a settlement near San Antonio. It still smelled like a new house, the odors of brick and mortar and sawn timber melded into one. And why shouldn't they have a fine house? Why shouldn't the boy,

Tom, grow up in it? These people had once been owned by other men, then broken apart on a whim, the baby and mother separated from Charlie for eight years, until one day he'd found them again.

Hub would never forget the look on Charlie's face when he ran out of the church tent five or six years before where he'd gone looking to buy a blanket—Hub was standing outside Fort Sill with Sarah's father and some other men, counting their money from the just-completed cattle drive when Charlie ran yelling, "My boy! I found my boy!"

She sat him down and brought him a dipper of water. "You want something to eat?"

"No. No, thanks. I need to talk to Charlie." Rose was probably over thirty, but she still looked like a girl, thin and energetic, her face expectant, as though something interesting might happen at any moment. She and the boy had spent those eight years with a preacher and his wife in San Antonio while Charlie roamed Louisiana and Texas searching for them. Hub had never seen bitterness on her face.

"Him and Tom's off a ways, clearing some pasture land. Cedar's so thick on parts of the place the grass can't grow."

"I reckon they'll be in for supper."

"Tell you what—I got a dinner bell at the back door loud enough to wake up them politicians over yonder at Austin. You just wait a minute and I will get them boy's attention."

The bell set the dogs to howling and they had to have a few shouts from Rosabelle before they quieted down. She went into the kitchen and rattled pans. It was early, all right, but they'd be wanting something to eat.

Charlie and Tom rode in and tied their horses out front, surprised to see Hub waiting for them. Both were soaked in sweat, their clothing dark with it, their hands smeared with the sap of the cedars they'd been cutting. Charlie's hand was sticky when Hub shook it. The boy had doubled in size since that day in the Indian Territory, tall and muscular from ranch work. Fourteen now?

"Ain't seen you for a while," Charlie said.

Hub told him what had happened.

"I guess you lookin' for something to ride, then."

"If you can spare it."

"I got them two plow mules running loose. We could saddle one, but he'd sit down in the first creek you crossed. Don't think I can recommend it. And I can't loan you my horse. Tom, can you loan Speedy to Mr. Anderson, here?" He grinned at Hub. "That's a name Tom give him."

The boy was reluctant, but out of politeness said, "Yes, sir."

"Good. Thank you, son." To Hub he said, "Speedy's been saddled all day, but they just been grazing loose while we worked, so he ain't tired. I guess you wanting to hurry on, ain't you?"

Rose's voice from the kitchen—"Not before some supper."

Hub could smell something good cooking, the hint of smoke from her stove. "Not before then," he said.

"You didn't ask me why I can't loan you my quarter horse."

"Why, no. That's your business, Charlie."

"It's because I'm gonna be riding beside you."

CHAPTER 3

THEY trailed half the night, the full moon giving them plenty of light to see by, and stopped to camp where the horses had crossed the San Saba.

"Expect they out somewheres between here and the Concho," Charlie said after the grounds had settled in Hub's pot and they'd poured themselves a cup each and leaned back against the saddles that would serve as their pillows in a little while. The night was chilling down and Hub was glad Charlie had brought along two blankets.

"Used to be big mustang country out there," Charlie went on. "You can see to next January and that's how them wild ones like it."

Hub said, "Yes, I've been on some horse hunts myself. They'll stay on the open prairie long as they can; won't hardly go into timber except to hide out."

"They about finished, though. Run down, penned up, killed off. You may have to shoot this stallion yourself to get that mare back."

"That would be a shame if it comes to it. It's something I don't want to do."

"Naw, but...I seen one of them stallions pull a man out of his saddle one time. Man roped him, and the old boy just turned and come back and got the man's leg in his mouth and

pulled him down. Would have stomped him to death somebody hadn't put a bullet between them wild eyes."

"Can't be many of 'em left, I'm thinking. We may be chasing
one of the last of the mustang stallions in Texas," Hub said. He
finished his coffee and set the cup down, rubbed a hand across
the burn of smoke in his eyes from the campfire.

"I think you're right. *The* last one, maybe."

Hub laid his head on the saddle, pulling the gray blanket up
around his chin, thinking of his wife and baby girl and missing
them when he tipped over into sleep.

The San Saba was an hour behind them when the sun
came up. Breakfast had been cold biscuits and cold river water.
Daylight brought a little warmth with it, a little hope, and Hub
began to believe they'd come on the stallion and his herd before
the day ended. Tom's gelding didn't have the springy step, the
easy gait of Hub's mare, but he'd do. Plenty of bottom, didn't
seem to tire under the steady pace. Despite the name Tom gave
him, though, he was not fast. Not fast enough to catch that
stallion when he ran.

But if Hub could get within sight of the manada, if the
mare could see him, smell his scent, she might bolt away,
outrun the master stud and come to him. The plow team, the
jenny and the line-back dun—now that was another story. He
wasn't likely to have them in harness again. Not without an
all-out effort, a capture of the whole bunch. And that would
take more men, more preparation, probably the building of a
pen with wings to guide the herd inside it. This stallion had
caused him a bunch of sure enough trouble.

They were north of Fort McKavett, the army outpost on
the San Saba down in Menard County. Charlie knew the fort

and the country around it. He had spent two summers there looking for Jim Bowie's lost mine, following the markings cut into the heavy timber along the river by the Spaniards a long time back—the Spaniards, many believed, who had smelted silver into ingots shaped like lizards, iguanas. He had looked hard for a long time and then stopped looking. Didn't expect to try again.

The map that Bill had given him before the old man died had taken Charlie in one circle after another through the region where he'd come across many a rattlesnake, but no silver. Hard to say why he'd kept after it so long. The treasure was real—Charlie knew that from the ingots Bill had given him; enough to buy a ranch, a house, some cows.

Los Iguanas, The Lost San Saba, The Lost Jim Bowie, whatever you called it, Bill had been that man's slave, claimed to have seen it, had silver to prove it, silver hidden away long ago by the Indians who massacred the original Spanish miners.

No, he'd worried over it too long, and given up. His real treasure, the only one he cared about now, was his wife and son, and they were riches enough for any man.

CHAPTER 4

A jackrabbit bounded out of the grass a hundred yards away, paid no mind to the two riders, head down and hind legs pumping in hard earnest; an animal built for speed—then a blur of motion in the sky, an impact, a scream from the jackrabbit. And silence. Hub and Charlie reined their mounts forward, curious, neither of them sure just what it was they'd seen.

The struggle was ending as they rode up; the jackrabbit was still kicking, but his life was over. A small hawk, the blur of feathers from the sky, sat on him, the talons of one foot embedded in the rabbit's head. The bird seemed not to notice the men and horses intruding on its hunt. It had already begun tearing into the still-living flesh with its hooked beak. This was not the kind of hawk that killed off their chickens—in fact, Hub couldn't remember seeing the likes of it before. No matter. He pulled his peacemaker and was about to shoot it when somebody yelled.

"He's over yonder," Charlie said.

Appearing out of a shallow cut in the prairie a rider came at full gallop waving his hat in the air. Hub held off pulling the trigger, watching the rider come closer. A young man in dusty cowboy clothing, the horse under him blowing hard from exertion, reined in and dismounted and stood over the two small animals on the ground. He glanced up at Hub and Charlie.

"Howdy."

Hub holstered the pistol, wondering what he was seeing.

Charlie said, "I ain't never watched a show like this one before. You reckon we still asleep?"

The cowboy looked up again. "This here's a huntin' falcon," he said. "Belongs to Mr. Duncan. He'll be here in a minute." To Hub he said, "I'm pure glad you didn't shoot her. And you can be glad, yourself."

Another rider, then, at a slower pace, came toward them through the grass. The horse was a solid black; the man wore dark trousers and a billowing scarlet shirt of shiny cloth. On his left hand was a leather glove with a cuff that reached his elbow. His hat hung behind him by its chin strap. A saddle and bridle of black leather were set off by silver decorations that caught the sunlight and spun it back at them as the horse came forward. Dismounting, the rider ignored Charlie and Hub.

"The hood, Elmo," he said to the cowboy. His voice sounded high and strange, the accent not quite right. The young man produced something from his shirt pocket and handed it over.

Through it all the small bird had kept a death grip on the jackrabbit, tearing and pecking at the flesh. It stopped when the leather hood came down, loosened its grip and allowed the man to lift it onto his glove. Hub saw leather straps dangling from its legs and heard the sound of the bell attached to one of them.

The stranger looked up at Hub for the first time and spoke as if he were continuing a conversation. "The trick is to let her have just enough of it to keep her interest in the hunt, but stop her short of fully appeasing her appetite." He grasped the leather straps in the gloved palm of his hand and the hawk sat on the gauntlet, gripping it with the same talons that had so easily penetrated the jackrabbit's skull.

English accent.

Hub said, "My name's Anderson. This here's Charlie Boone. We're here by accident, and it was something we've not seen before."

"Yes, I may be the only falconer in the country just now. It's a rare sport. You should learn it."

"Just what kind of bird is that, anyhow?"

"Peregrine falcon." He lifted his arm, showing her off. "Some say they're the fastest bird in the sky. I believe it's true."

The cowboy named Elmo held the man's stirrup steady for him as he mounted the black, balancing the small predator, settling into his seat. He took the loose reins in his right hand and spoke to Hub again. I'm Robert Duncan. You gentlemen are riding across land I have under lease from the state. You are welcome to cross, and I trust you'll not molest Duncan stock as you go."

Hub took off his hat and leaned an arm across his saddle horn. "No worry there. We're tracking a stallion that stole a mare from me two nights ago. A mare and two work animals. He's brought them out here somewhere, and I aim to get them back."

"I know the horse you speak of. In fact, anyone who owns horses in this area knows him. He's the last of his kind. We've gotten rid of the rest—had no choice, really. Those wild stallions made it impossible to maintain one's own remuda, raiding as they did practically every night, driving away valuable animals. I believe this one has mares of mine even now, thoroughbreds brought from Kentucky at great expense."

"What's this boy look like? Might help if I know what to watch for."

"Typical Spanish pony. A dun with black markings. Rather small, actually, but don't be misled. He can run away from you until you kill the horse between your legs and then a second horse, and he will still be running with that infernal pacing gait of his."

"Well, despite that I mean to get my mare back." Hub had first seen her years ago on his walk home from the Louisiana battles after Lee's surrender. Starved and lonely, she had followed him; then, when he could walk no longer, had carried him the last miles. He wouldn't give her up without a fight.

"Your quarry has a name, by the way. It has to do with the fact that he's the last of his breed on this prairie." Duncan reined his restless mount in a circle as he spoke. "He's called *the sundown stallion* out here. He'll make a fine mount for the man who captures him alive. Like most vaqueros, I won't have a mare or gelding under me, only stallions. A man's horse says something about him, don't you think?"

He didn't wait for a reply, raked a siver rowel across the black's flank and the two men rode away without a farewell.

Hub and Charlie watched them until they disappeared behind a rise in the prairie.

Charlie said, "Don't ask me what I think about all that."

"I won't. Fact is, I already forgot it."

They went on their way as black vultures began circling in the air behind them.

"There come the cleanup crew now," Charlie said, glancing up. "It's just a skinny jackrabbit, I know that. But don't it seem wasteful to you?"

Hub ignored the question.

"No sir, don't ask me what I think about it."

CHAPTER 5

THOUSANDS of years before the hoofs of wild horses tracked this soil, a decline in the earth's surface caused rains to run westward in the direction of what would someday be called the Concho River. In the running of the water westward bits of soil went along, eating deeper into the surface except at the spot where accident or purpose had placed a granite shelf. In time, to a watchful eye, the granite would have seemed to rise up, but that was not the case. In fact, the earth around it was carried away. The end result was the same—a high mesa of rose-hued granite in the midst of green prairie.

Erosion had constructed an inclination on the northern side of the rock, where winds and rain beat on it hardest, making it possible for a man or an animal to climb to the top. And it was there, on the treeless mesa, that he spent many hours every day, his manada always in sight below, grazing in safety under his eye. In every direction the land led away open to him. Any movement, any threat, caught long before it could harm them.

The figures moving now far to the south were going away and caused him no fear. They had first appeared on the western horizon, one man riding, another walking, and though the mustang's first instinct was to race down off the mesa and push his herd to another place, it had quickly become apparent that there was no threat and he had settled down to watch. They diminished slowly and disappeared finally, and once again, as far as the stallion could see, was nothing but a prairie of green grass beginning its golden turn toward winter.

* * *

They boiled another pot of coffee. There was plenty, because Rosabelle had insisted Charlie take along some of what she'd ground up for them in her new machine. It was a tempting spot they'd found, and if not for the lost mare Hub would have enjoyed staying put there for the night, although there were hours of daylight left. The horses they rode had led them there, scenting water and pulling in that direction. Tall trees, cottonwoods mixed with a few Spanish oaks and live oaks surrounded the spring of water, and a half-dozen granite boulders made convenient back rests. There was plenty of shade, and many hoof prints of unshod horses. A watering spot for the wild ones, probably. The night past had been chilly, but the afternoon was hot, with swarms of tiny gnats circling their faces. Night would be a relief, but it was hours away.

A few yards from their resting place a rock tumbled loose and rolled and Hub's hand went to the grip of his pistol. He saw a horseman, and another man walking behind. Strange sight—a rawhide noose around the walker's neck, its other end wrapped around the saddle horn.

"Good afternoon," the rider said, lifting off his hat. He was a Mexican, but his words held little of the Spanish accent. "All right if we share this water with you?"

Charlie stood up. "Course it is. Get off your horse and rest a while. We about to leave anyhow."

Hub said, "There's still some coffee left, if you're so inclined."

"Believe I am, thanks." He took a cup out of his saddlebag.

"Your friend, too, if he wants it."

The stranger smiled at Hub. "No, he only drinks water." The man at the end of the riata had made no effort to speak, no move toward the spring. His eyes were on the ground. Hub noticed that his hair was long, almost to his shoulders. He wore no shirt, only a pair of trousers that looked too big for him, and was barefoot. His skin was tanned dark as a boot.

A quick swallow of the coffee and the rider put his cup down on a rock and took the riata loose from his saddle horn, clucked his tongue a couple of times and led the other man to the edge of the spring. The dark, shirtless fellow got down on his knees and drank, with deep slurpings at the water. While he drank, the rider tied the riata to a sapling and found his coffee again.

"Strange, no?" He smiled at Hub over the rim of the cup.

The drinker got up and faced away from them, standing straight, his weight on one leg, the other knee bent and resting.

"Does he talk?" Hub asked.

"Not to me." Interesting how you couldn't tell this man was Mexican without looking at him. He wore regular clothes, but a sombrero sat on his head. He seemed to be friendly enough, but he carried a pistol at his waist, and that bore watching. It was turning out to be quite a day.

Hub said, "Excuse my question, mister. Hard not to be curious."

Charlie spoke up. "Well, I ain't ashamed to ask, not that you got to answer me." Another swallow of coffee. He shook his head and said, "I don't mind. I'm Mendoza, by the way. Born in Mexico, raised in Texas, vaquero outside, gringo inside. Or maybe it's the other way around. I ain't sure."

Charlie identified himself and Hub.

"This man," Mendoza pointed his cup at the other, "I captured a week ago running with a horse herd in New Mexico."

"Running with 'em?" Charlie said.

"Look at his feet." He got up from the crouch he'd assumed. "Here, I'll show you." He lifted the foot as you might lift a hoof and showed the bottom of it, ran his fingernail across it. "Hard as that saddle horn. Don't nothing bother him."

"Them horses live on grass," Charlie said, "what's he live on?"

The stranger shrugged. "I've got him to eat mesquite beans. Seems fond of 'em, but that wouldn't get him through the winter. I guess I'll wait for winter and find out."

Hub said, "Him walking thataway slows you down. Why not put him up behind you? Or maybe catch a horse for him to ride?"

Another shrug. "Tried it. He won't get on one. Won't stay if I put him up."

"Well, where you walkin' him to?" Charlie wanted to know. "'Scuse me for askin' but I got a special interest here, having walked at the end of other men's ropes myself. So to speak. If this ain't slavery, I don't know what is, and I believe it's against the law."

Hub walked over and offered the silent man his last biscuit, but the offer was ignored. On impulse he reached into the morral and brought out a little corn, held it in his hand. The man sniffed a couple of times and turned to it and held out his own open hand, which Hub filled, then put the corn into his mouth and began to grind it with his teeth.

Charlie said, "What you got's a crazy man. That dry corn will break his teeth. Let me ask one more time, where you walkin' him to?"

Eyebrows rose under the sombrero. "Not your business, friend."

"I'm about to make it mine. This man think he's a horse is one thing—you acting like he is, that's another thing."

Hub understood why Charlie was getting rubbed the wrong way by this affair, but he didn't want to lose the day to argument or worse. His mare was still lost somewhere on this prairie.

He said, "Mr. Mendoza, you're probably right and it ain't our business, but you can see why my friend here is taking exception to what you're doing. If you could just clear our minds a little as to the treatment this man is getting, why, we can go on our way. I've lost my mare to a rogue stallion and time is important to me."

Mendoza looked at him as if his words had made an impact. "You are lucky you met me, then. I know where the manada is. I saw your mustang stallion before I got here. He's in his querencia, watching all the prairie. You can't approach him in daylight. He stands on a high mesa and can see everything."

Charlie said, "What's a quer...whatever it was you said?"

"It don't translate. It's his place, that's all. It's where he is at home, knows the water, the weather, the ground under his feet."

Hub said, "You talk like you've hunted horses before."

"All my life, yes. I worked as a mustanger all over the Llano Estacado, up into Indian territory."

"From what I can see, that work is about done with."

"Oh, for a long time now it's finished. For two years I've made my living hauling buffalo bones to the railroad in Abilene. What a slaughter those men made with their big guns. Killed off the buffalo for hides and let the meat rot on the ground, so the Indians out there starved with nothing to eat."

"What do they want with bones in Abilene?" Charlie asked him.

"I don't know for sure. Fertilizer, I think. Grind 'em to a powder for farmers to put on their crops. Somebody told me they make buttons out of 'em, too. All I know is it pays six dollars a ton. You ought to see the stack at the railroad yard."

Hub told him, "I'd be much obliged if you could point me in the direction you spoke of."

"I will. And here's the story of that silent man over there— to the south of us is a cow operation belongs to a man named Duncan."

Charlie spoke up. "I believe we met the gentleman this morning."

"And was it a pleasant meeting?"

"Wouldn't say so, no. He was huntin' with a bird."

"That's the man I'm speaking of. He's a falconer, as he calls it. He is a man with much money, earned ferrying cotton from Mexico to England while the Americans fought their war. He married a Mexican woman and settled here. A very beautiful Mexican woman, take my word, and when her parents died her brother came here to live with her. Yes, this man you see was once my dearest friend. But he went to live with Estrella and her husband five or six years ago. Life with Robert Duncan didn't suit him for reasons I can guess, and one day he ran away. Estrella came to me and persuaded me to go and find him. This is the brother and I am taking him home to his sister. After that, I return to the hauling of buffalo bones and this man is free to go his way."

"You're certain he's the brother?" From Hub.

"Oh, yes. I've known him and his sister since we were children. My father was a foreman on their big farm until he left that life and brought us north. This man and I have sat together in places where music played and had our glasses of tequila and told each other stories. He was my friend. Who knows? He may be again."

"I reckon there's reward money in all of this," Hub said.

Mendoza shrugged. "They are very wealthy. Why not?"

There were few landmarks, but enough moonlight to follow the directions Mendoza had laid out for them. He'd offered no further explanation of his unlikely journey, or the unlucky man at the end of his riata who seemed to think himself a mustang. Not long after he had given Hub and Charlie directions to the mesa Mendoza had led the other one away, hoping, he'd said, to reach the Duncan headquarters by dark.

"We need to make ourselves a plan," Charlie said after they'd ridden in silence for a while. "That stallion gets a sniff of us he'll take off, make no difference it's night time."

Hub said, "The advantage we have is that we can get in closer than in daylight. I don't want to spook the herd, though. We're not set up to start a chase that could go on a week, and there's no pens that I know of that we could drive 'em into."

"Sounds to me like we ain't got no chance of catching your mare. Makes me wonder what we doing out here."

Hub laughed softly. "I should have borrowed the mustang man. Maybe he could get in the herd and catch her."

"Or maybe he could run off to New Mexico again. That was a strange thing, I'm telling you. Never heard of such before, man thinking he a horse. And that Mendoza feller didn't give us the whole story, neither."

"Well, Charlie, here's my thoughts on it—I know all I want to know. Now then, there's just one way to get this job done and that's capture the stallion ourselves."

"You think we can?"

"I believe there's a way, and it will take us both to work it."

CHAPTER 6

THE stallion had been awake and in motion long before dawn. He had trotted out from his herd in all directions, snuffing at the wind, searching out dangers, finding none. He had pushed his way through the mass of bodies, the mares and the few mules and geldings that accepted his leadership, found a female in season and mounted her. She resisted briefly, until he came down on all fours and bit her fiercely on the withers and remounted.

All his manada had settled into grazing now and he ceased his vigilance long enough to crop some grass for himself. One of the mares nickered and when he raised his head to look, the other animals had stopped grazing, their heads uplifted, eyes wide, showing white, waiting for his reaction.

The figure was so far away the stallion, even with his near-perfect eyesight, had to look carefully to be sure, but it was a man, all right, riding one horse, leading another, coming toward them at a slow trot. The herd master bellowed his alarm cry and took off in the opposite direction, the mares at his heels. A hundred yards farther on he circled to the rear, rounded up the two or three that hung back and forced them into the racing mass. The rider came on at a slow, steady pace.

They ran for miles, stopping once for water, and now and then to rest. But no matter how far they ran, after a while the rider would appear on the horizon, still coming toward them, and they would run again. The sun was high in the sky when the stallion began pushing them in another direction—a gradual arc that would take them back to the point where the chase began. He did it out of instinct, out of experience, and out of his longing for the mesa and the grasses around it. It was a flaw in the mustang makeup that caused a wild herd to always do that—always return to the piece of ground that was their territory. Or, if flaw is the wrong word, it could be said that it was a part of the mustang makeup that man learned to exploit.

The day went on and still the rider came, but he was farther and farther behind them, and in the afternoon when the sun dipped lower and it seemed he would chase after them forever, he gave it up and they saw him no more.

The stallion had won again.

He was easier on the others now, pushing them ahead, but not with teeth or hoofs, using only his presence, their fear of him, to keep them moving.

There was still daylight on the prairie when they returned, but shadows were long. The herd spread out to rest and graze before night. He wanted a clear look, wanted to be sure the threat was really gone. He trotted alone to the north side of the mesa and began to climb over the granite rubble at the foot of it.

Something happened then that had never happened before—the gravel in front of him erupted and a naked man stood in his path, swinging an arm above his head and there was a sudden touching of his neck. He reared back and felt the touch become a hard restriction that cut off his breath. His half-strangled cry was more from rage than fear.

Hub scrambled out from under the stallion's hoofs. The animal came for him, lips rolled back and hard teeth exposed, but Hub had rehearsed the capture for hours while he lay beneath the decomposed gravel hoping he was right. A boulder had tumbled off the mesa long ago and it was just a jump for him to get behind it to a spot where he couldn't be reached. When the stallion reared again the loop on his neck tightened and began to choke him down. The game was done.

Charlie had made the riata years before from the hide of a steer, the hair soaked off in lye, cut in a circular length two inches wide, softened in water and stretched and twisted until it was tight and hard, then greased with tallow into a flexible loop that could hold anything walking. The end was tied in a knot and buried in a hole Hub had dug with his knife, packed solidly then hidden with more of the loose gravel off the mesa. Buried like that it could be pulled out straight up, but from no other direction.

They'd taken every precaution—Hub had doffed his clothing and turned it over to Charlie, then washed himself in a creek and rolled in dust to cover his scent. In the hours after sunup while Charlie pushed the wild herd he had prepared the hiding place, careful to keep it looking undisturbed, leaving nothing to catch the stallion's eye or his nose. This had been the only hope of catching the stallion and recovering his mare, and if it hadn't worked she might've been lost for good.

It was a relief to stand upright again. He left the plunging animal, edged his way around the rock out of range of tooth or hoof and began watching for Charlie. The manada had run a half a mile away and stopped, unsure just what to do, all the screaming and carrying-on disturbing their composure. Some of them had dropped their heads to graze. The sun was going down and the golden light smeared its colors over the grasses and over the group of animals. He spotted a bay that was watching him and whistled. It was the mare, all right. She came toward him at a gallop.

CHAPTER 7

AFTER the first night alone, not sure when to expect Hub's return, Sarah had carried the baby girl and walked the few miles to the Bent T, her father's ranch where she had lived all her life except the young years as a Comanche captive, and now as Hubbard Anderson's wife. She wasn't sure how many miles it was, but it took her until noon and she had begun the walk after breakfast. Ben Turner was happy to see her and his grand-daughter, of course, but he was concerned, too, at the news. No telling where the chase had taken Hub or what kind of danger it represented.

Alta was there, busy in the kitchen, and her mother, Turns Away. The name didn't translate very well out of the Comanche and Ben had taken to calling her Turna. The youngest girl, Rabbit, had reached adolescence now, growing tall and pretty, like her sister. John and Falling Rock had let their horses loose in the rock-fenced pasture and were walking toward the house when she got there.

John kissed Alta before he spoke to Sarah, and Sarah wondered if she would always feel the little sting of jealousy. The boy had been married for over a year now and it was time she got used to it. John was gaining a little weight, turning into a muscular man. She remembered how he had been all those years growing up, a shamed, drunken half-breed boy without hope. It wasn't until John had learned he was the son of the war

chief Two Hawks that he began to change and become himself.
Why had she tried so hard to keep the secret? Telling the truth
at last had made all the difference. She'd been only four years
old when the raid occured, her mother killed while Ben was
gone. She grew up as a Comanche, became wife to Two Hawks,
then on a trip through the hills to Mexico the band had been
attacked by a group of settlers led by her father. Her rescue had
cost Ben Turner an arm, and cost Two Hawks his life, and she'd
kept the secret until John's seventeenth year out of fear that
their neighbors might seek revenge on the boy. Two Hawks had
been a gentle husband, but a savage warrior.

A small band of Comanches, avoiding the Fort Sill reservation, had lived in a cave two days ride from the Bent T. They
had learned about John and wanted to make him their chief,
had carried him away. Hub had been there then, hunting wild
cattle along the Llano he'd planned to use for stocking his
Brazos Valley ranch. He and James Harper had joined the hunt
for John, and they'd found the boy unharmed, in the company
of a few friendly Indians and Charlie Boone. In the days that
followed, John had fallen in love with the Comanche girl, Alta.

He had been determined to save Alta and her family, had
brought them here with the hope his grandfather would accept
them, allow them to stay. And it had worked out even better
than Sarah had believed possible. Falling Rock had given up the
Comanche way out of love for his family; put off the breechclout, put on the white man's trousers, learned enough of the
language to get along, did a hard day's work every day alongside
John and Ben Turner.

And so the family was saved from the Fort Sill reservation,
but there was a never-mentioned sadness among them—Alta's
younger brother had chosen to stay with the hills and prairies,

find another band of Comanches and continue on the path of war with the whites. For a long time they had talked of the young man named Chaser, then slowly ceased doing so until he lived in each one's memory, but was mentioned no longer.

John took Marie from Sarah's arms and cuddled her, sang her a song while she stared at him. Her hair could be called strawberry blonde, somewhere between Sarah's blonde and Hub's bronze.

Sarah recognized the song. "Alta's been teaching you." It was a Comanche lullaby.

"Yeah. I have to be ready when we get one of these, you know."

"When you get one? Johnny, you make it sound like it's something you ride to the store for."

"You mean Harper don't sell 'em?"

Ben said, "Let's sit down here and have our dinner. It's not often we get the pleasure of you at the table, Sarah."

They took turns holding Marie while they ate. Talk at the table was pleasant, family matters, some gossip, the afternoon of work ahead. Sarah had little appetite despite her long walk, couldn't stop thinking about Hub, wondering where he was and when she'd see him again. She watched her father across the table. Ben seemed happy, adept at eating with his one arm, the left sleeve pinned at the shoulder. He'd lost the arm to a crushing rifle ball one day long ago—the day her son was born, the day her husband died, the day she returned to the white world. Ben always said it was a trade he had been glad to make, though years had passed before he understood why the war chief had fought to the death that day. The old man had cried when she at last turned loose of the secret she'd held onto out of fear. Funny thing about secrets—nobody had cared. They'd all forgotten, and when the truth was out it had become a healing truth, rescued her son from aimless self-destruction and blown apart the barricades she'd erected between herself and the iron-haired man sitting across the table. Made them a family again.

Now that John was older she could see his father in the angles of the young man's face, hear the warrior's voice in the laughing voice of their son. When her husband died that day she had thought her own life over, as well, her memories of the brief childhood in this house gone and the nomadic life of the prairie the only one she knew.

Some of the memories had come back—her mother trying to hide her from the raiding Indians, and then the woman's body still and bloody on the ground as the four-year-old was carried away, bits and pieces of the white language, but the essential life force inside her had dried up like dew in the sun.

The sadness of spirit had never left her until another day just a few years ago when she'd stood in this very room, holding James Harper's ring in her hand, hearing his pleadings of love and marriage, unsure, afraid to speak, afraid to move, until through that western window had come the distant sight of wild cattle and a tall, bronze-haired rider and she had known the answer then, known the story of her life as if she'd read it in a book. She'd given James back the ring and waited for Hubbard Anderson to discover what she already knew.

CHAPTER 8

THE stallion reared and raged, choking himself down. Nothing Hub could do but wait to slip in close and loosen the riata. After what seemed a very long time the animal went to his knees, his breathing loud and labored, eyes wide and rimmed with white.

Too bad Charlie wasn't back to put another loop on him, but Hub knew he had to take the chance now or the horse would choke to death. The head was down, the black mane touching the prairie soil. Hub came in behind him to grab the leather loop and pull enough slack in it to make breathing possible again. Then he was out of hoof range before those eyes lost some of their desperation, before the push and pull of air became silent and the lips turned back to show teeth.

The stallion had learned quickly. When he stood up he didn't rear again, understood the purpose of the thing that held him. Hub admired the intelligence from a distance, the clean lines of the wild body, the sweep of mane and tail never shaped by a grooming hand. His own overflow of feelings had begun to ebb now after the boredom of the long wait, the hope and fear, the exhilaration when his planning turned out right and the loop had gone over the mustang's head. Everything was settling now, and back came his memories of wife and child and the need for home. His own querencia.

"Well, you pretty thing, what am I gonna do with you now?"

The mare had come to his call and though he had nothing to lead her with she had followed at his heels back to the shade of the mesa and stood in the shadow caused by the lowering of the sun. The sky held few clouds and out of the direct sun the temperature had dropped. The air felt sharp and clean and he smelled earth and stone, felt goosebumps on his arms and legs. The stallion stood in one spot, rigid, eyes straight ahead. Now and then a muscle trembled.

When Charlie rode up leading Speedy he took in the situation with a quick glance, raised the hat off his head and said, "You are one smart man, Hubbard Anderson. I figured to find you naked and afoot and with evil disposition."

"Shut up and throw me my clothes, Charlie. I'm cold."

They shifted the saddle off Speedy and onto the mare. He put the bridle on her that he'd brought from home and now the two men were able to get loops on the stallion's legs and stretch him out, but you'd have thought the entire Comanche nation was on the warpath from the noise and dust they raised getting him hobbled. Hub went in close and got a short rope around the neck and the other end attached to a front fetlock. Now, when the stallion was let loose he couldn't run or he'd throw himself down. They could take the loops off and let him free to fight it out with the rope.

Once on his feet again, he laid his ears back and charged Charlie, but even before the quarter horse could spring out of danger the mustang's head went down and he rolled onto his shoulder and over on his back. Hub saw a spot of blood where the shoulder had scraped rock going down. The horse lay there without trying to rise. He raised his head and looked out at the prairie and made a sound in his throat that broke Hub's heart and made Charlie turn away from what they were doing.

There was little to eat or drink, but the two men made do with a small fire that reflected heat off the granite uplift. They spent an almost sleepless night watching the stallion, who did not attempt to stand again. All night they smelled the smoke of the fire and the dark risings off the sage and grasses of the prairie around them.

At first light Charlie was on his feet and walking toward the downed animal.

"Where you headed?"

"He plans on laying there and dying. I'm gonna get him up."

"Look out, now. You'll get hurt. Wait for me." Hub struggled to get his moccasins on, but Charlie didn't wait. He bent low to the horse's head as though whispering in his ear and there was no reaction. Then a handstroke down the handsome face. Charlie bent lower and huffed his breath into the stallion's nostrils, waited a moment and did it again. He worked a rope hackamore over the ears and tugged gently.

"Come on now, boy." He stroked the neck and head some more, leaned his weight against the horse.

"He'll bite a chunk out of you," Hub said. His voice felt lost in the swirl of morning, a breeze too light to turn a leaf.

"No, he won't. He's all right. Come up, boy."

And all at once there he was on his feet like he was lifted from somewhere high above them. Standing and looking at Charlie and then at the herd of mares in the distance, raising and placing down again the tethered foot.

"Learned that from the Comanche," Charlie said. "Best horse people in the world. Horse smell your breath—and mine ain't all that sweet this morning—but anyhow they smell it and they know you."

They stood back from the mustang and he took a tentative step in the direction of his manada, but something stopped him there. His head was low, held down by the short rope, but he wasn't restrained from walking. He appeared to just choose not to, turned away with his back to everything, looked up at the top of his mesa.

Charlie and Hub walked nearer the fire, stood warming their backsides, both quiet. Hub heard the insistent, round notes of a whippoorwill getting ready to close shop for the day. He said, "Well, you're in this with me. What do we do with him?"

"You the man caught him."

"And couldn't have without your help. I'd say we're partners in this studhorse."

"You want to take him home with us?"

"No, I'll just catch my jenny and lineback dun and give you my half of the stallion, Charlie."

"Them mares'd follow us if we hitch him up to Speedy and lead him slow."

"Well, I'm willing, if that's what you want."

"No, it ain't."

"That's a surprise, now. Here I was thinking you'd jump at the chance to ride a stallion. Most vaqueros do, you know."

CHAPTER 9

THE mule and gelding were easy enough to catch and the stallion stood still when they rode back to him. It was quick work to set him loose. He pawed with a foreleg, seemed to sniff for the scent of the missing rope, slowly understood and walked a few steps, then trotted away. The mares had burst in all directions when Hub and Charlie roped out Hub's two strays. The mustang had hours of work ahead, rounding them up again into a manageable herd.

"We had some luck catching him, Charlie. Guess nobody's tried what we did."

"Yeah, but he won't be caught like that again."

"I'm glad we turned him loose."

A hundred paces away the stallion collapsed, hit the ground so hard he seemed to bounce, and then the sharp report of a rifle split the air close by. It took a second before they understood what had happened.

Charlie said, "Some fool has shot him." Then the sound of men shouting, hoofbeats coming closer. Hub took to his saddle and saw Charlie do the same. They rode out from under the mesa's edge. There were five men on horseback. Hard to know what to expect. He drew his pistol and let it rest on his lap hidden from view by the saddle's pommel. The horse hadn't moved from the spot he'd fallen.

The leader's black horse and the silver winks from his

saddle told Hub soon enough who this was. And right behind him, waving a rifle high, was the man Mendoza.

"Creased him," Charlie said.

"Or killed him."

The riders dismounted, hovered over the fallen horse, two of them roping his hind legs together. Duncan looked up.

"Gentlemen," he said.

"He alive?" Hub wanted to know.

Mendoza spoke up. "Like I told you, I'm a longtime mustanger. I don't miss."

"The trouble here is, you never could've got close enough to shoot."

Duncan stood up straight and smiled. "The facts seem to argue differently, friend. We did get close enough."

"That's only because me and Charlie caught him last night, and decided to turn him loose just now."

The Englishman seemed to think that over for a second. "If that's true, which I doubt, it was a foolish act on your part and doesn't change anything. I want another stallion, and this one is mine."

"Stay on your horse, Charlie." Hub holstered his pistol and stepped off the mare. Something he hadn't felt in years, the old war-rage, was boiling up in him, black and stench-filled.

Duncan came to meet him. "Yes, I called you a liar." The smile never left his face. "You wish to take offence? Many have."

"Get away from the mustang, all of you." Hub said. The words felt like bullets in his mouth.

The men did as he said, backed away. He heard the lever of Charlie's rifle, the cocking of pistols from among the strangers. Duncan stayed put in front of him with that smile under dead eyes, too close—men didn't stand that close to you unless they meant harm.

"Pistols? How are you with a Bowie Knife?" The mockery in his voice matched the look on his face. Hub's open right hand came up from his hip, caught Duncan above the left ear and put him on the ground beside the stallion. Hub heard the snap of metal all around, but for him there was only the man on the ground and the black desire to kill him.

"Whoa, Hubbard, slow down, now." Charlie's voice seemed distant, barely penetrating the curtain that had dropped around Hub. But he heard it, and understood, and in moments the understanding replaced the blackness with a flash of memory— his daughter's face, the sound of Sarah's laughter, the smell of supper on the table.

Duncan got to his feet and retrieved his hat. The smile was gone. Every one of his men held a revolver and the muzzles were pointed at either Hub or Charlie, who still sat his horse with the rifle ready.

Mendoza said, "Be a shame, dying over a wild horse."

Charlie said, "Got to die over something."

Duncan regarded him from a few paces. "I should have expected an act of that nature from a man who rides a mare."

"What sort of act you prefer?"

"I told you. Guns, knives, the honorable settlement of differences. The slap of an outraged woman? My word." The mocking smile was back. Duncan's face was red and beginning to show bruising.

Hub pictured the faces again of those waiting at home for him. And for Charlie, too, back at his house. "Put your rifle away, Charlie."

"I do that, they just shoot us, anyway."

"Not so!" A protest from Duncan. "We're not barbarians, after all. You men, lower your weapons."

Hub remounted. The Englishman said to him, "You don't think this is finished, do you? These men are witnesses to my word, and I will have satisfaction for the insults you've handed me today."

The rage had passed now and Hub felt the familiar hollowness, the looseness in his body that always followed combat. He started to reply, changed his mind, laid a rein on the mare's neck.

They headed back toward the mesa to collect Tom's horse, and the other two that were still hobbled. Hub smelled the smoke of their little fire, down to a few smoldering coals now. Morning was full on them, the way home well-lit and waiting.

Charlie said to him, "I hope you didn't back off on my account."

"No, but I've changed, I guess. I kept thinking about them that's waiting for us."

"That Duncan feller gonna pester you."

Hub sighed. "No way around it, likely."

When they were almost out of sight of the mesa behind them he noticed the mare glance back for a moment. He ran his hand along her neck and said, "I know, gal, I know."

CHAPTER 10

ISIDRO Mendoza said to Duncan, "I've done my lowdown piece, like it or not, so I think I'll move on myself, you don't mind. You and these men here can handle the horse."

"I don't think so." Duncan kept watch on the disappearing riders. "You're the catcher of mustangs, as you've bragged. I need you to break this one for me."

"That wasn't no part of the deal. We wouldn't even be here if I hadn't misspoke about seeing the stallion. I brought back Estrella's brother, like I promised." Mendoza had regretted telling about the strangers from the moment it happened back at the Duncan ranch.

"And well paid for it, too, in money and my wife's... gratitude."

"Don't know about that, sir. I ain't seen her nor spoken to her. Not since she sent me looking for her brother."

"Worth your life to do so, Mendoza. All right, you alerted me to the mustang's whereabouts, creased him as advertised, without killing him, as I expected. Good enough. Here's your money. Now go your way, so long as it is not my way."

The downed horse began moving his legs, trying to raise his head as Mendoza rode off and the men turned their attention to getting Duncan's new property on his feet. Mendoza traveled north around the mesa until it sank below the horizon, then made a gradual arc to the west, then south. He kept a distance of two or three miles between himself and the other two riders going that direction, and he kept the silence.

He rode for hours, knew he was back on Duncan's lease now, knew he was in trouble if they caught him here. This was a man's true danger—not the things you expected, bullets, wild animals, the unexpected fall from a great height—no, something softer, gentler, far more dangerous, far more compelling. Just that once, that precious once, and yet he had never forgotten Estrella's kiss. Yes, it had been only a kiss in friendship, without passion, but it had kept him warm many nights through many years on empty prairies.

The moment the figure walked out from behind the boulder he knew he was lost.

"Still a dirty liar, I see." Duncan raised his rifle and fired.

Mendoza hardly heard the explosion, absorbed as he was by the searing pain in his belly and a tumble from his plunging horse.

He tried to wrap his body around the pain, comfort himself somehow, and could not. Couldn't raise his head, even to look his killer in the eye. The lever action rang, something hard poked at his head.

"Gut-shot," he heard the Englishman say. "Want a quick one in the head, or do you prefer to lie here and let it leak away?"

He couldn't speak. Anyway, what could you say to a question like that, he wondered, as if it had been addressed to someone else. It was not so bad here on the ground. He liked it, in fact. The smell of it, rich and wild, the intricate design of grass and leaf, the movement of an ant near his face. It would be good to live like the ant, in soil like this, to burrow deep into it and breathe its aroma all around you as you slept.

"No," Duncan's voice again, "I won't hurry you along. Tonight when I lie down beside Estrella I want to remember you gut-shot on this prairie, dying a slow and painful death. Now, where is my money? In one of those saddlebags, I'll wager." The words became fainter as Duncan walked away. "You should have known, Isidro, no man can touch my wife and live to remember it."

"Somebody shootin'," Charlie said.

"Long way off. No telling who."

"We still on that fool's land, ain't we?"

Hub laughed. "I don't know. He seems to think the whole state's his."

"Mostly is, I reckon. Him, and the rest of 'em like him. Leasing state land, makin' deals in Austin, pattin' little fat men on the behind and stuffin' money in their pockets."

"I guess it won't ever change, Charlie. They're like prairie dogs—run 'em down one hole, they pop out of another one."

"Talkin' about prairie dogs, I'm nearly hungry enough to eat one. We could stop a while and fix a bite."

Hub glanced at the sun. Almost down. "Yeah, but we can get home in a few hours if we don't stop."

CHAPTER 11

IT was a great disappointment to Sarah when Ben halted the wagon in front of her house. No light anywhere, Hub not home. No telling where he was or what had happened to him. Her arm and shoulder were numb from holding the baby as the wagon team drew them onward in the deepening night.

"Looks like our man ain't back yet, honey." Ben sounded tired. She should have waited til morning instead of letting him do this. But there were chores that needed seeing to, chickens that had not been fed, and somewhere out there in the dark a jersey cow that still had to be milked.

Marie went down without a sound while Ben lit a lamp in the kitchen. She said, "I really have to milk the cow before anything else. You look tired, Papa. Stay the night with me before you head back."

He nodded in agreement and said, "I'll brew us some coffee and see about a little supper. I'd milk that cow for you, but you know one hand ain't enough."

She laughed with him despite the cold knot in her stomach. The note she'd left lay unread on the table. She crumpled it and threw it in the stove. Suppose something bad had happened to Hub? That fear was always in the back of her mind. She walked to a corner of the room and picked up one of the heavy boots he'd left standing there. It helped a little just to hold it, as though she were holding on to him. "He wore the moccasins I made for him."

Ben must have heard the longing in her voice. He came over and put his arm around her. "That man of yours is tougher than the boot in your hand, Sarah. He'll be fine."

After she carried the lantern outside Ben built a fire and in a few minutes had coffee boiling and the house warming up. Easiest thing to fix this time of night was some bacon and eggs, he decided. He got out the lard and rounded up the rest of it. Sarah would have to make the biscuits. That was something else that needed two hands.

He heard Sarah's voice. Was she talking to herself? A man's laugh, the closing of a gate, wood slamming on wood, the dry rattle of a chain. Good news, then. Things would be all right now. The two came in the back door holding onto each other, the coal oil lantern swinging from Hub's free hand. Its light was no match for the new and welcome light in Sarah's eyes.

* * *

Isidro Mendoza had not yet died. That must be true, since he could plainly see stars along the horizon, the dark intrusion of mesquites in silhouette against the full moon. It would be good if he could raise his head higher so that his eyes could take in more of the stars, the estrellas, but something about the movement caused pain that was like the quick ripping of cloth deep inside him. The odors of the ground he lay on had changed since darkness had come. Gone the dry, thin essence of the day, replaced by something full and rounded, made whole by the light's absence. Perhaps he would change that way, too, when his light went out. Something like the padres taught once, when he was young, and when he listened to such talk. Listened to promises. Believed them.

He welcomed the shadow that fell across him. *Cougar? Wolf? Tear me apart, then. Eat this pain and take it from me. On this night of the full moon I offer up my flesh.*

The soft nosing at his hip, a murmured question from his horse's throat. A smile found Mendoza's lips. "I'm glad it's you," he said, surprised that the speaking caused no pain. "Hard to believe, no? Caught me with my pants down, all right, me thinking how smart I was the whole time. But never mind. A dying man ought not to talk so much."

The horse almost straddled his body. Come to protect him? Maybe. It was very nice to think so. The two of them had been together a long time, and they had always treated each other well. "I hope somebody finds you pretty soon," he said. "You could eat better if that bit was out of your mouth. I would do it if I could."

And then he reached out and touched a trailing rein. It hurt to move, but not like before. He moved the other arm, as well, and put his hand inside the stirrup that hung above him. "If you will kindly lower your head maybe I can do you a service."

But the head didn't come down and he was tired from holding on. He was about to let go of the stirrup when a thought came past so swiftly that he almost didn't catch it. *Pull myself up?* But he hadn't enough strength in his arms, and his legs didn't seem to work at all. The bullet had injured his backbone, probably, like you'd stop a running pronghorn when you hit him in the right spot.

Anyhow, the saddle was no better place to die, even if it was closer to the stars. *But maybe I won't die. Don't hope that, don't think it. But maybe. Okay, you horse catcher, maybe.*

The man who had shot him, that Duncan, the Robert Duncan who had done it was breathing just now the scent of Estrella in a feather bed, laughing at him, relishing the knowledge that Mendoza lay here dying. Not dying? And here came anger. He had forgotten about anger, and here it was again as though it could be used, as though there were time ahead and a use for it. He had forgotten anger and the strength it brought him, the strength it gave a man in combat when he fought for his life, fought the night for his life.

Mendoza was halfway up the side of his horse but had no memory of getting himself there, held by nothing except the muscles of his arms, and the pain through the middle of his body was so great it caused him to moan and the horse to shy back, pulling the useless legs along the ground.

"Whoa, boy, whoa now, whoa now," he whispered through the clench of teeth, and the horse heard the familiar voice and stood there quietly again until the man could gather enough muscle and rage to haul himself over the leather seat and hang there. After a time he turned lengthways, feeling pain that was the color and consistency of drying blood and push himself partially upright, his dead legs hanging down.

The reins would have to trail on the ground. He couldn't reach them. The horse began to walk, each step like a fist into Mendoza's belly. And the animal seemed certain of his direction, now and then lowering his head to the ground. That wouldn't do. He was trailing the scent of Duncan's horse. Wouldn't do at all. Mendoza put his right hand on the saddlehorn and stretched his left arm far enough to grasp the leather bridle strap behind the horse's ears, and he used it to pull the animal's head away and got him moving another direction.

CHAPTER 12

THE bed in which she lay awake was not made of feathers. The mattress was filled with cotton, cotton such as her father had grown once, picked by peasants and hauled out of their fields by teams of mules in high-topped wagons that lifted white lint into the trees they passed whenever the wind came up. And under the mattress were steel springs that squeaked at movement on the bed. A candle burned in a corner of the room, a pleasant scent of burning wick drifting from it. She liked the movement of shadows on the walls. The room was cold, but two quilts covered them and kept them warm. Robert Duncan had eased quickly into sleep, tired from the chase after the mustang stallion. Her husband didn't often seem happy, but tonight he'd been different, almost pleasant.

She slid from the bed onto the cold floor and felt the chill on her bare feet below the hem of her flannel gown. She took the candle, was careful opening the bedroom door and walked to another door farther down the hall. She opened the latch. The room inside was dark but the glow of the candle flame outlined the figure of her brother standing beside the bed, head down.

"The bed is for sleeping, Felipe," she said in a whisper. He looked up at the sound. She came close beside him and touched his cheek with her free hand.

"Please don't be crazy anymore, Felipe. That you should be my brother again."

Robert's voice startled her from the open door. "He will never be your brother again, Estrella. His mind is gone for good."

Felipe turned away from them and moved to a far wall, out of the candlelight.

"You see? He doesn't want your light, or your love."

Robert was completely naked, as though the cold meant nothing, showing his body, his muscles, his maleness, inviting the world to look at him. "It's you he's afraid of," she said.

"And why should that be? I've done him no harm." That, she knew, was only a half-truth. Robert had never cursed Felipe or hit him with his fists, never used a club against his head as was often the case when her husband worked with his horses. But the man's cruelty was something that harmed those around him even when directed elsewhere. She herself could never bear to watch the assertion of his will on the things he owned. As he wished to own her. As he perhaps did.

"Where did Isidro find him?" She said.

"I didn't ask."

"Did you pay the money you promised him?"

"Yes, I did."

"Where has he gone? Did you harm him?"

"He was alive when I saw him last. More than that I can't say. Do you miss him?"

"We've talked about this too much already. One small kiss, a meaningless touch for a man I knew as a child. You grant me not even that much freedom. Your unforgiveness is an insult." She forced him out of the way and closed the door behind her. She could hear the soft padding of Robert's feet as she followed the candle flame back down the hall to the cotton mattress and warm quilts of their bed. Just that one small kiss on the lips of a childhood friend stopping for a visit after so many years, and then the unending jealousy.

Far behind their house, at the end of a path paved with fieldstone hauled from off the prairie land, the whitewashed outbuildings shone like chalk in the light of the full moon. Beside the largest building, a barn that held hay and corn and stalls for the keeping of horses, was a circular pen built of heavy logs buried endwise in the ground and reinforced by braided rawhide that circled it horizontally on the outside. In the center of the pen the solitary stallion stood with his nose attached to a snubbing post. He could not have lain down even if he'd wished. Entrance to the pen was through an opening barely wide enough for a horse, barred by three more heavy timbers now so that even had the stallion been able to pull loose from the post he could never have kicked his way free. And there he waited for morning.

CHAPTER 13

HUB woke up still hungry, remembering their quick supper of the night before and wanting more of the same. Sarah was up already. She had let him sleep a little longer, but he had to move now, stretch out the soreness in his legs and arms with work. Had to see about the mare—those little cuts from the stallion's teeth could get raw without some salve on them. And he had to hold his baby girl for a few minutes and be grateful for the good things that surrounded him.

Sarah was at the door, fright on her face. "There's a horse out back, Hub, a man on the ground. I think he's dead."

Ben was already kneeling beside the man. Hub got there with only his pants on, barefoot, limping from grassburrs.

"He ain't dead," Ben said, "But may as well be. From the blood it looks like he's been shot in the belly."

"I know this man. He's the one creased the mustang I told you about."

"What you want to do? Ought to get him out of the sun, I guess, take a look at the wound."

"I can ride to Junction City, but it will probably take a day at least to get the doctor out here."

"Yes, but it smells like blood poisonin' already. That nasty stink? Man'll be dead before then."

Hub let out a long sigh. "I know the smell of it well enough from the war. Not much we can do, then."

"No, but I never been one to sit on my backside and watch a man die without trying to help him. Get Sarah. She knows things I don't."

She met Hub halfway to the house. He went inside and finished dressing, peeped at Marie asleep in her cradle and came back to find Ben and his wife settling the wounded man on a bed of hay under the roof of the wood shed.

Sarah showed no hesitation in unbuckling Mendoza's belt and pulling his pants partially down for a better look at the wound. "The bullet hit the belt buckle and splintered, see? One piece went sideways, in and out beside his hip, and the other one straight in under his navel."

Ben said, "And didn't come out. No blood on his back. It's still lodged in there."

She felt the ashen forehead. "Fever. And his heart's beating real fast. I've seen it before." She got to her feet and faced Hub. "I need two knives. That Arkansas Toothpick of yours would be a good one, and another one with as long and thin a blade as we have. Sharp. Just as sharp as you can get them. And two or three yucca leaves. The whole leaf, mind you, from the tip of it to the end." He heard the baby cry.

"Marie's awake."

"I'll see to her. You do what I asked you, and hurry."

He found a yucca not far from the house, dull green, the long leaves stiff and sharp after the cold night. He used his folding knife to cut three of them loose, pricking his hands on the sharp points. He wondered about their purpose as he carried them back.

It took him a few minutes to hone the knives Sarah wanted and while he got it done she used a pair of scissors to clip the tip of each yucca leaf almost to the edge, then pulled each one down so that a fiber remained attached to it. Needles and thread. Ben held his granddaughter, talked to her, quieted her crying. The infant reached out to touch his beard.

Hub said, "You planning to cut into him?"

"Yes, water's boiling on the stove. Bring it out here and put the knives in the fire. I need a red-hot blade."

"Sarah, are you sure—?"

"Why, no, Hub, I'm not at all sure. Get the water."

He stabbed the knife blades into the coals of the cookstove and hurried the kettle of steaming water outside.

Sarah soaked a clean cloth and used it to swab away dried blood from the wound. "Bring the Arkansas Toothpick first. The double blade will be of use." When he brought it she took it from him and said, "Won't take long to cool down. I'll need you to bring the other one then and put this one back in the fire."

He took Marie from Ben and carried her on his shoulder as he went back and forth, trading red-hot blades for cooler, bloodier ones, rinsing the blood away as best he could. The heat cauterized the flesh Sarah cut into, holding back bleeding. He understood the purpose but silently questioned the effort since the man's death seemed certain. The smell in the woodshed was hard to take. He watched Sarah pull a loop of gut into the light and use one of her yucca needles to sew a tear closed.

Ben said, "It's leaked out, though. It's inside him, and that's what will kill him."

"Maybe not." She looked up at Hub again. "Can you bring me another kettle of water? Not boiling this time, but warm. And put some salt in it, just a pinch or two."

He had used up all the water in the house and had to go to the well and draw another bucket, and it took two arms so

Marie cried in her cradle while he did it. Aggravation was setting in—his role as fetcher of knives and water was tiresome and the whole matter probably futile, and after yesterday's trouble he didn't feel all that friendly toward the man. Plus, he was hungry.

Sarah took the kettle from him and poured it all at once directly into the open hole she'd carved in the man's belly, then said to Ben, "Help me turn him over so it can drain out."

Hub waited for the next order and didn't like it when it came. "Listen to me, now. Ride to the river, straight out from the house, and go east along it to where that little creek empties in it. You know what I'm talking about?"

"Surely do."

She seemed to understand something from his tone. "Please don't be mad at me, Hub. I didn't mean to sound so bossy."

He heard something from Ben that might have been a laugh in other circumstances. "I ain't mad. It's all right, go ahead and tell me what you want."

"There's a tiny pool of water that backs up beside the creek. Probably thirty or forty paces from the river."

"Okay. I've noticed it."

"There's green slime grows in it, right on top of the water."

"What are you talking about?"

"Bring me a bucketful of the green slime."

"I know you ain't crazy, Sarah, but that sure sounds like it."

"And hurry up with it."

He rode Mendoza's horse. Saved saddling the mare. It took half an hour, maybe closer to an hour for the trip, and it was hard carrying the heavy bucket through the brush along the river.

She scooped the mess from the bucket with her hand and

ladled it into the wound, forcing it inside. He looked at Ben. Ben shrugged and managed a smile.

"Let's get some blankets on him," she said. "I'll make breakfast, Hub, and you'll have to ride to Junction City for the doctor."

CHAPTER 14

IT was late in the afternoon when he left the Sheriff's office and rode the mare down to Harper's store. Bigger, now that more people had moved out here, with a new tin roof on it. The doctor couldn't get out there today—like he said, there was more than one life and death situation waiting on him. Tomorrow, though, before noontime, and yes, probably for nothing, but you do what you can.

Question now was whether to go home, which meant more hours on the road for a tired and hungry man, or stay in town and bunk with James Harper. They'd spent the better part of a year together in an E Company tent on the Red River during war times—before James got his stiff leg from a Yankee ball. His old tentmate seemed to carry no ill feelings about Hub's good fortune, as he shouldn't. Hub hadn't even considered courting Sarah until after she turned down James' proposal. Still, after all this time, James hadn't found another woman. But like the doctor said, you do what you can.

A woman was asking questions about a piece of merchandise. Hub looked at the display of rifles and sidearms in their places behind the counter. New models, and more of them than James used to carry. Must be prospering. The woman was a blonde, like Sarah, with a wise look to her, like she'd been around some, but pretty, and a trim figure. She seemed familiar, as if Hub had seen her before, but he couldn't place her. Smiling up at James like that. James smiling back.

Leaving, she paused long enough in the doorway to look back and wave to James. Perfume marked her trail through the aisles.

"Who's that?"

James blushed. "Name's Clawson. She goes by Jezzie, short for Jezebel. Now, who'd give that name to their daughter?"

The last name was one Hub remembered. "She got a brother?" Raiford Clawson had saved his life years back. It was after they'd tracked John and the Comanche band to their hiding place. The rest had gone back home, but Hub had stayed out hunting cattle when a wild bull gored him off the mare and nearly killed him

"She's never said."

"But she lived here once?"

James' color deepened. "Yeah. She was with that police captain you shot it out with. His mistress, I guess you could say. But she's put all that behind her."

"What's she doing here now?"

"Now, Hub—you can't have this one, too." James laughed, but there was a message in what he said.

"She's all yours, my friend. I was just wondering."

"She's put in a little dress shop down by the bank. Stuff for women, you know? She brought a wagon load from California and says she's about sold her stock out and may have to go back for more."

"You need some time off from this store. Why don't you take her out there and make sure she comes back?"

"I've thought about it. Maybe I'll offer. I'll need somebody to supervise things while I'm gone, though. Maybe you'll volunteer."

"No, I'd make a sorry clerk, James. I imagine there's others you can call on." He told about the wounded man and about the mustang, and as he talked he decided he'd been gone from home too much lately and long ride or not, he would sleep in his own bed tonight.

* * *

Robert Duncan carried an axe handle and a saddle blanket into the pen and told the two ranch hands to barricade the opening. One of them was Elmo, who cared for the falcon, the other man someone whose name Robert didn't remember.

"You ought to let us help, Mr. Duncan," Elmo said. "That's a mean old stud."

But Duncan had decided this was his job, his *challenge* as he'd told Estrella at breakfast. The stallion would be broken before nightfall, and would know Robert Duncan was its master. Why had he once thought he needed Mendoza's help? All morning it had been his pleasure to remember the man falling from the horse, the smell of gunpowder clean and bracing in the cool air. The hours of suffering and slow death. A ring of buzzards around him now, tearing away at the man's hated flesh.

"You men go on to your work. This is private."

He circled the horse at a safe distance and stood an arm's length from the snubbing post. His body was tensed, ready for whatever move the horse made.

Nothing. The stupid animal didn't even look at him, dull eyes fastened on the ground. Not look at Robert Duncan? He raised the axe handle and brought it down in a slicing arc between the stallion's ears. And got his reaction.

Before Robert could move, those dark hoofs were in the air above his head, hot breath pluming in the cold air, white teeth lunging for him, jerked back by the short rope, but not before the man had fallen backward, axe handle flying out of his hand to clatter against the timber fence, saddle blanket tangling at his feet.

Duncan looked at the barricaded entrance and dared eyes to be there watching. Lucky for the cowboys, they'd gone. The unbroken horse pulled against the rope around his neck, making it taut, choking himself, his breath wheezing, until he remembered and eased up.

The Englishman got the axe handle again and tossed the blanket away.

"Come on, now," he said, crouching, inching forward, driving the club into a raised foreleg and then backing away. The mustang screamed in pain, tried to lunge, began choking and eased up again. Duncan went in and delivered another hard blow to the head, his temper flying now.

The horse tried to fight back, but couldn't get enough freedom to move. He got the club between his teeth once and held on, tried to bite through it, but the man pulled and twisted it until it came free. The hoofs that had murdered other stallions, had stomped the life from wolves and cougars, could not prevent the pain, the onslaught, because of the rope and snubbing post.

Blows landed again and again against shoulder, flank, bony leg, hard skull bone. Something about the light changed, gone on one side. The smell of blood was everywhere, pouring from the cuts. All knowledge, all instinct, all desire, torn open and destroyed.

"Fight me, will you? Here's one for you. And here's one more!"

The stallion was exhausted, but he would have fought on, as he had fought all his life, except that his spirit left him. Except that he experienced what had never before occurred—he was defeated and knew it.

Estrella Duncan moved through her house tidying things, straightening a picture on the wall, putting a cushion back in place, picking up a straw left by a broom. A faint noise came to her attention. It had been there for a while, but hidden behind her thoughts, her wondering about the fate of her friend, Isidro, her memory of his kiss, her denials to Robert.

The noise sounded like muffled cries and she followed them down the hall to her brother's locked door. Earlier she had fed him boiled corn, the only thing she could get him to eat. Maybe he was hungry still. Tears on his face.

"What's wrong?" She hurried to him and he turned away. His body moved as though receiving blows, as though pounded by fists. He rubbed his hands over his arms and legs, he looked at her and agony was on his face along with tears. And he spoke. With a voice not heard by anyone in years.

"Please let me go. I will die here."

"But what's happening, Felipe? What's wrong?" Was he coming back at last from the far place his mind had wandered to?

He shook his head, cried out in pain.

"The stallion. Make him stop." The last word dragged thin, as a child might beg.

It made no sense to her. "What are you saying? Make the stallion stop? No, no, I see. It's Robert? Hurting the horse?" And though she did not yet understand she left him there and rushed out of the house and along the limestone path until the sounds from the timber pen told her what she'd find.

"Stop it, Robert! You're killing him!"

"Shut up and go away," he told her, aiming a kick at the animal's ribs, missing.

"No, I won't!" And she scaled the barrier, dropping to the bare ground, her dress billowing out, snagging a moment on rough bark. She ran between them, falling against the stallion, smelling the sweat and rusted iron of his blood, facing her husband. She might have been harmed, but the massive body she leaned on remained still, offered her no threat. Her breath was deep, fast, not from exertion but from the fear of what she'd done. Almost without thought. Fear of what would happen now. Never had she opposed Robert Duncan. Because of love, in the beginning, then out of the knowledge and fear of him.

Duncan lowered the axe handle, let it touch the tumbled soil at his feet. He spoke in an almost gentle manner. But the gentle manner did not allay her fear.

"What are you doing, Estrella?"

A question she had no good answer to. "Felipe...spoke to me."

"Felipe doesn't speak."

"But he did, and he feels the pain of this poor horse. He cries out from the pain."

"Oh, please, Estrella, are we back to that again? It is still preposterous. Get out of my way."

"No. I won't! Look what you've done, Robert. Look at this wild creature you've beaten senseless. Will he love you now? Is that what you want with your bloody club?"

An ugly oath spilled over his lips like dirty water. He dropped the axe handle where he stood, climbed the barrier and was gone. She turned to the trembling horse and ran her hands over his back, the shaking of her own hands and arms burning up the fear that filled her veins.

Felipe waited for her outside the pen and walked with her to the house. She had forgotten to lock his door. "I will get warm water and wash the blood off the poor horse," she said, as though this man had not gone crazy and run away with a herd of wild ones for two years, as though he understood the things she said.

"And some salve on the cuts," he said. "I remember salve."

"Oh, Felipe," she said, stopping to embrace this person who seemed to be her brother once more. "Where have you been? Where have you been?"

Out of the stables Robert Duncan rode his black hunter northward, the hooded falcon perched on his arm.

CHAPTER 15

"UH oh," Charlie said. "Looks like somebody cut that wire." They were on foot, carrying a crosscut saw and a double-bitted axe, the horses grazing loose somewhere close. They'd been at it since early light, and as the boy had told his mother at supper the night before, it seemed like you cut one cedar and two came up in its place. Grass didn't grow under the cedar needles, and the low evergreens sucked up the water, starving the hardwoods that Charlie wanted to keep for shade over the cattle he intended raising.

Tom beat him to the broken wire and called back, "Yeah, they cut it clean. There's more, too, more than just this."

And he saw that his son was correct. Somebody had done a job on his fence. Looked like whoever did it had pulled staples out of his posts, cut the wire and then rolled it back and tied it off. Hundreds of yards of it. At least the posts were still in the ground—he wouldn't have that expense, anyway, just the wire to fix. What that would cost and where the money would come from he couldn't imagine. There was no money to fix this with unless he sold off some of his stock. And by the cow tracks it looked like some had already wandered through the cut space and would have to be caught and driven back. Good that the brimmer bull was close to the house in his own separate pasture. There was no way Charlie could replace him.

Tom was first to notice the riders.

"Daddy?"

Charlie's heartbeat picked up, but he kept his voice calm. "Come on back here with me, son." There were three men on horesback, off his property, sitting quietly in the shadows of the trees, one of them rolling a cigarette, the others simply watching him and Tom. They were not men he knew by name, but their faces were faces he had seen on the streets of Junction City.

His guns were with the horses. He said, loud enough for the men to hear, "How y'all doing today?" None of them made an effort to answer.

"Go find them horses, Tom. Bring me my rifle."

The boy started off and one of the watchers said, "Stop right there, now. We don't need to be hurtin' no kid today." Tom stopped and stood there quietly.

"All right. We both stopped. What is it you want?"

The same man said, "What we want is for you to pull up your wire and get off this homestead."

"I'm not provin' up a homestead, mister. I bought this land, dollar a acre. It belongs to me."

"A lie, I would guess, but even if true it just means you stole the money from some decent white man."

Charlie whispered to Tom, low enough that the others couldn't hear, "When I say run, you run. Try to get to the horses. I'm right behind you."

Louder, he said, "I ain't done nothing to bother anybody. Why you men runnin' us off?"

"We'd of done it long ago except for the bluebelly soldiers you been hidin' behind. Now they've pulled out of the fort things are gonna be made right. People like you are back to bein' what you've always been."

Charlie let the words settle. "Well sir, I been many things—I was born a slave." He reached out and took the axe from Tom. "I was a Seminole for a while in Loosana, and a Comanche for about two years here in Texas. But I ain't never been—run, Tom—white trash!"

He heard the boy's quick feet, threw his crosscut saw into the cedars and as the riders came out of the trees he sent the double-bitted axe end over end into their midst. A horse screamed and a pistol went off. Missed him, but they had stopped for a second or two and he hadn't, running for his life.

Two of them were spitting cuss words and pushing their horses after him. A stand of the cedars cut him off from their sight and here came Tom with the rifle. Charlie caught it in mid-stride, levered a shell into the chamber, turned and knelt, aiming high, and fired in the air above the first rider who came into view. The bullet went over the man's head, but it was enough for him to throw his horse back on its haunches, sliding to a stop. The wire-cutter had his pistol out, but Charlie had his face dead center in his sights, and he knew it. The second rider stopped behind the first.

"Come on up beside him so I can see you, mister. Tom, that other one's trying to sneak around us on foot. Get the pistol and watch for him."

"I got it right here, Daddy."

"Good boy. Anything moves out there, shoot it. You men, now, you put them six-shooters on the ground. Just drop 'em right there."

The front rider spurred his horse and it jumped straight at Charlie and he shot it in the chest, had to, and already felt bad about it, but the other one was on him now, and he let the horse live and shot the man out of the saddle. A pistol barrel was at his head. He couldn't turn in time and thought he might die while

Tom watched. There was an explosion behind him and the gun at his head went spinning. Tom was holding onto the handle of the old .44 like it was a snake and looking sick.

A voice came out of the woods. "We gonna kill you, Boone."

"Come on, then." He fired the rifle at the voice. Branches snapped and leaves crackled under running feet.

"He's gone," Charlie said, taking the heavy pistol from his boy. He held Tom close, felt his chest heaving, said, "I'm proud of you, son." He could barely hear his own words, the gunshots still ringing in his ears. "You saved my life just now. You know that?"

"Yes, sir." A whisper.

"It was him or your daddy, don't ever forget that. We got some hard days comin', that's for sure, but don't never forget it was them or us."

"I won't forget."

They hung the two bodies over the remaining horse. There was a blood trail in the direction of the road, so he had wounded one animal with the axe, and the third man was riding it, on his way somewhere with a mouthful of lies.

"It's a miracle one of you didn't get hurt," Rosabelle said, hugging them both, staring out her open door at the corpses on the strange horse. "Why can't we all just run, Charlie? Away from here. We could hide til everybody forgets about us."

"No, I done enough hidin'. This is our land. Didn't we say we are home? Ain't that what we been telling each other? We didn't break no law. Them men's dead because they tried to kill us, me and Tom. The only way to stop 'em is just what you're lookin' at out there in the yard."

"And who'll believe it? All that gossip about us, where we got the money for everything, how we think we better than people in town. You've heard that talk. Who's going to believe you?"

"You're right, Rosabelle, far as that goes. Not many. Not after that third wire cutter gets through tellin' his stories."

She sighed and dropped her head. "All right, Charlie. Tell me what to do."

"Stay here today and hope for me. Tom stays here, too, and I'll keep him out of it if I can. That other one didn't see what happened, he'll say I done it all. I got to take 'em in soon. Can't look like I'm trying to hide from the sheriff."

"There might be men on the trail. They could hang you from a tree before you ever make it to town."

"I'll stay off the trail, Rosabelle. I'm goin' to Hub's place first. If he's at home he'll go with me. Between the two of us, won't nobody hang me."

"And how we know about you, huh? How me and Tom going to know, here in our fine house, what is happening to our man? We lost you one time already, Charlie."

"I'll get word to you. If the sheriff don't throw me in jail I'll be back tonight, maybe. But I promise you this—you won't lose me again. Tom, I'll leave the rifle here with you. I don't think nobody will come to bother you before I get back, but if they do the dogs'll raise a racket. If they threaten you or your mama, stay in the house, bolt the doors, and tell 'em you got a gun. They can't shoot at you through these brick walls. And listen to me, now. If one comes through the door or a window trying to harm you, then you do just what you done for me today. And don't think twice about it."

CHAPTER 16

HUB was splitting firewood. Time to lay in a store for winter. Past time, really, but other things had kept him busy. The day had warmed a little and he worked with his shirt off. He liked the feel of exertion in his arms and belly and back. And he liked the repetition of the work, the smell of the fresh wood, his thoughts free to wander as they did over the happenings of the day.

Hard to know what to tell you, the doctor from town had said. *You put what inside him?* And Sarah had been embarrassed and gone in another room, unwilling to say more about her Indian ways.

And the man had been shaking his head still, and talking to himself as Hub had helped him carry Mendoza to the doctor's carriage and secure the still-living body under the seat, wrapped in a warm blanket.

Sarah hadn't said anything else about it, and he'd been reluctant to bring the incident into conversation until they sat down to their mid-day meal. When she passed the cornbread to him she'd held the platter just out of his reach looking thoughtful, while he smelled the steam off the hot bread.

"White people think they know all there is to know. What I did for him kept him alive and the doctor thought it was just superstitious nonsense."

He stretched enough to reach a piece of the bread. It burned his fingers. "He didn't say that, exactly, Sarah." There was fresh butter from the Jersey on the table. He spread some on his cornbread and watched it melt away.

"You know as well as I do what he thought about it." She got herself a piece of the bread and buttered it.

"Well I believe the same as you. You saved his life. For a while, anyhow. It may not have been a save that lasts, though. A man shot that way, I never saw one live very long, and I've seen plenty."

She'd taken a little comfort from his belief, and he was grateful the whole thing was ended. There was Mendoza's horse to think about, his rig, but that could wait until time told the whole story. He sat another log on its end and split it down the middle with one blow.

And then he saw Charlie Boone riding up from the back. He hadn't come the quickest way, by the old Fort McKavett road that went past a half mile south. He led another horse that carried a load.

While Charlie was still a long way off Hub could see that something bad had happened. That load was two men, dead ones, judging by how they hung on the horse. He split one more log and put his tools away and stood waiting. First Mendoza, now this. Seemed like bad times had come upon them.

Sarah was unhappy about it, and who could blame her? "Oh, must you go?"

"Yes." The single flat word told her there was no argument.

"I guess you'll want Papa too, then."

"Well, he knows the sheriff and them other people, like the judge, better than I do. They'll give his opinion more weight than mine."

"Remember that he's not young. He'll be tired from his trip here."

"I will, Sarah darlin', but we have to remember that it's Charlie out there, and he's in trouble."

Ben Turner had finished an afternoon nap and was on the front porch with a cup of coffee when they arrived. He listened to the story. "Well, sir, Judge Potter's a reasonable man. The facts ought to shield you from trouble."

John decided to go along. Ben said to him, "Your mama is liable to be crossways with you and me both if you do."

"And that would worry me a lot if I was ten years old, Grandpa."

Second time in town in two days, Hub reflected as they crossed the north fork of the Llano at the shallow ford and started uphill to town, a town changed since he'd first seen it years before, come that day to visit his friend, James Harper, a friend he'd not seen since the terrible wound to James' leg in the Red River fighting, come to begin the task of rounding up wild cattle for his land on the Brazos. That had been the first time he'd seen Sarah and Ben, as they crossed the ford in Ben's wagon. And John, a drunken boy beaten by a bully police trooper—a trooper Hub had fought over the treatment of the woman and her son, and gotten a day in jail and a twenty dollar fine for his trouble. There had been no justice here then, no sheriff, no judge, just crooked self-serving martial law.

He wondered what kind of justice they would encounter today.

"Sheriff Bradberry's down at the cafe," the deputy said. He spoke with a German accent. "I'll run and get him."

Bradberry showed up a few minutes later walking beside

the deputy. He went first to the dead men and lifted their heads, looked closely at their faces, then motioned everybody inside. "Howdy, Ben, gentlemen. What's the story here?" He took off his hat, hung it on a peg beside the door and stood waiting. This was a different jail from the one Hub had spent time inside once. The other one had been a makeshift of logs with a couple of cells, and bunks for the police troop that had terrorized the county until Hub put a bullet through the late Captain Dugan as he threatened the Turner family on their front porch. Dugan had believed someone there was hiding silver treasure, and his greed for it got him killed.

"You know them men?" Ben said.

"Don't know their names, no. One of 'em I've seen a time or two at Harper's store. I think they worked on one of the ranches around here, but that's all I know." He turned to the deputy. "Gustave, if you don't mind, would you go see if James can come up here?" A quick nod and the man was out the door. "He may can contribute something about those two."

"Anybody else been here to tell about this?" Charlie asked him.

"What's your part in it?" Bradberry's voice seemed neutral, but that wasn't anything Charlie counted on to last.

"I shot 'em."

The sheriff looked surprised, glanced around at Ben, at Hub and John, and said, "Guess you better tell me about it. Let's all have a seat."

James arrived with the deputy before Charlie finished his story and stood silent in the doorway. Hub had watched him stop and examine the dead men before he came inside.

When Charlie reached the end of it Bradberry said, "Can you identify either of those men, James?"

"One is named Evans, don't know his first name. The other's a stranger to me. Evans works for a rancher by the name of McGee. Runs a spread north of your place, Ben."

Ben Turner said, "Walt McGee? We've swapped lies a time or two. He never seemed like a man that'd send his people off to do such a thing as this."

Sheriff Bradberry put in, "Walt's gone a little senile, is what I hear. A nephew of his come out in the summer from somewhere—Mississippi, I think—and took the operation over. I know because they went to Judge Potter and got up a paper that made it legal."

Hub said, "Maybe the nephew brought plantation ways with him."

The sheriff sighed. "Let's hope not. Charlie, I can't see a reason to hold you over. I know full well you ain't a killer. But I want all of you to sit a while longer til I can get Doctor Kountz up here for an opinion. He's the doctor here now, and I use him for a coroner when I need one." He sent the deputy to bring the doctor. James stayed a few minutes and went back to his store.

CHAPTER 17

KOUNTZ was in the middle of something with a patient and couldn't come for an hour. Bradberry said, "I got some papers need signing. While I take care of that business, why don't you men go have a cup of coffee. We ought to be able to finish up when you get back."

When they were out on the street Charlie said, "This is seemin' awful easy to me."

"Bradberry's an honest man," Ben said. "I think we can trust him."

"Not much choice. But say, y'all go on and have your coffee. I'll look around out here."

Hub said, "Don't you want some?"

"I've heard enough hateful things for one day. You know what'll happen."

"You want a cup of coffee?"

"Yes, I do."

"Come on, then."

And they went inside and sat around a table in the center of the single room. One other table was occupied by two men in town clothing involved in conversation. A man came out from behind the counter. He was a big man, with a broad, pleasant face.

"I'm sorry, folks, but we don't serve coloreds here."

Hub said, "This here is Charlie Boone. He's a good friend

of mine. Bring us some coffee." He said nothing more, and after too much silence the big man went back behind the counter and filled four cups and brought them out on a tray with a pitcher of cream and a bowl of sugar and spoons for stirring.

Charlie sat staring at the cup of brown liquid in front of him, breathed the steam, stood up and said, "I'll wait outside for you gents."

The coffee smelled good, but Hub couldn't bring himself to drink it. He looked at Ben and John, and all three stood up without another word.

"How much do I owe you?" He asked the man behind the counter.

"Nothing, I guess, since you didn't drink what I served you."

Ben laid a handful of coins down.

They strolled to the bank on one side of the street and then crossed over and started back on the other side, passed the little clothing store run by the woman James had said was Jezebel Clawson. Hub said, "Maybe I'll buy my wife something pretty. Wouldn't hurt either of you men to do the same."

Charlie said, "Don't know why I ought to buy anything for your wife. But go ahead. We right behind you."

Ben let the others walk in ahead of himself, then said, "Looks a little tight in there. I'll wait outside for you." Women's things—perfume, lace, bonnets, were things he stayed clear of. His wife, Sarah's mother, had missed pretty possessions out here. Sometimes she'd had a dress or shoes or a piece of furniture brought up from Galveston or San Antonio. The things in the store would remind him too much of her, remind him that he'd been carousing in San Antonio, drinking, acting a fool, when the Comanches came, stealing Sarah, killing the woman, the stock, burning what they couldn't carry away. Like he told Sarah once, he hadn't touched whiskey since, but it had already been too late.

They carried their hats, careful in the aisles between hanging clothes, all seemingly so fragile they might be torn apart by a rough touch. There were no other customers and the pretty blonde woman came to meet them.

"Good day," she said, "is there something in particular I can help you with?"

"We're all married men," Hub told her, "and maybe there's something we could take home as presents for the women."

"No doubt. Let me think, now."

Hub said, "A question, if you don't mind."

"Not at all."

"I saw you in Harper's store yesterday. He told me your name, and I was wondering—a man by the name of Raiford Clawson saved my life once. I never was sure what happened to him. Might you be related?"

"Oh, yes. He's my brother."

"I guess he's left the country."

Her eyes lost a bit of their shine. "He's in California."

"I thought that might be the case. Seems like half of Texas went out there after gold. Is he doing all right?"

"With Raiford it's hard to know. Sometimes he has money, but it escapes him fast."

"If you see him tell him Hubbard Anderson sends his regards."

"Your name is familiar. Are you the one who—?"

"Yes, I'm the one. The captain left me no choice. He was about to fire on this young man standing beside me."

She glanced at John, put a hand to her throat. "Oh, how frightening. Well, good riddance I say."

A small crowd had gathered in the street near the bodies, mostly men from the saloon. The horses were restless from the talk and movement going on around them. Hub put the scarf he'd bought for Sarah in a saddle bag and took a minute to pet the mare and soothe her down. These were the very men, the kind of men to start trouble.

The sheriff walked out of his office, looking around, and said to Hub, "There's Doctor Kountz now."

He recognized the man who'd come to treat Mendoza. Kountz caught sight of Hub as he walked up, appeared confused, stopped and said, "Your man is still alive."

"Well that's a wonder. Will he pull out of it?"

"Who knows? All I can say is that his death is no longer a certainty."

"Let me know the freight when it's done and I'll see you get paid."

"Is he a friend of yours?"

"No, sir. Just a man I met on the prairie."

The doctor put his hand on Hub's shoulder, nodded once and followed Bradberry into the office. The two cowboys had to be taken off the horse and laid out on the sidewalk, and they were a problem to examine because they were stiff and bent over from the way they'd been carried.

Kountz told the sheriff, "Looks like one bullet in the chest for one of the men, and the other took a ball in the head. Different weapons, I'd say. The head shot was something big."

"This old .44," Charlie said, indicating the pistol at his hip.

One of the idlers in the crowd was the town undertaker, a short, wide man with an expression on his face between compassion and cheer that seemed to move either direction at will. He wore a dark suit and a necktie. Bradberry sent him and four volunteers off with the bodies. The rest of the crowd drifted away after that and the street settled into its usual quiet.

Bradberry said, "Whose horse is that you brought 'em in on?"

"Belongs to them, I guess," Charlie replied. "Ain't mine."

"Well, you can leave it with me. The last thing I need to ask from you is go over to that other desk in the corner. Can you write?"

"Just my name."

"Gus, let him tell it to you again and you write out what he says."

The deputy motioned to Charlie. They sat down and began.

There was a light in the window and he knew Rose and Tom were inside, probably awake and afraid, uncertain of his fate. The dogs set up their usual noise until they heard his voice and quieted down.

"It's me," he called out from the yard and the door slammed open and there was a rush of feet and her hands pulling at him, pulling him out of the saddle, arms around him, the boy standing close behind her.

She brought a lantern and they stayed with him to the barn through the unsaddling. Tom put corn in the feed trough and they walked through the mill of dogs into the house. There was food she had prepared in faith and kept warm for him, and they sat near him while he ate it. The road home had been dark under the new moon, just a tiny whisker of light hiding up there in the stars. And when it had come time for Hub to pull off the road, leaving him alone for the last stretch he had been afraid. Couldn't call it anything else. Afraid something would get between him and the sight of these two. But nothing had. Nothing but nightbirds and wind.

Rose listened to everything he had to tell without comment.

Charlie lingered with the boy while Tom got himself ready for bed. He wished to hold back the dreams that might come to the child who today had killed a man. He remembered his own dreams years ago when he'd taken the life of the plantation overseer, a man who had chained him the day Rose and Tom were stolen from him, whipped him like a dog as a warning against running after them. War's end, the long butcher knife, and the overseer's blood on his hands—blood he'd left there for days. The woman's words, I sold them to Rafter in New orleans, the smirk on her face, the bullet hole in her forehead that he hadn't meant but had put there anyway. He knew about the dreams that could come, all right.

Rose helped him off with his boots. He felt too tired to walk from chair to bed. She said to him, "Don't think all this is over, Charlie, cause it ain't."

CHAPTER 18

FELIPE dozed on his feet. Yes, people slept on beds, but he had not done so in such a long time that it would be an abnormal thing for him. And how was it he had come here? It was difficult to remember much, but Isidro had talked to him, he was sure of it, had brought him back here. Did they get drunk on tequila? No, that was some other time.

The pain was still with him. He would like to give it back to the stallion, but knew he could never do that. He only took it in. It was the pain in that stallion that had brought him back from the great space in which he had lived for so long. And it was pain—the pain of animals crying out under the hands of the man with Estrella down the hall—that had made him crazy. *Am I crazy? Yes. No. I have been but now am not.*

Far from the room where Felipe stood, the mustang which was a mustang no longer, but a captured horse like other horses, leaned against the timber wall that held him in, as far from the snubbing post as he could place himself. When he closed his eyes to rest he remembered the sensation of touch, the hands that had washed him earlier in the day. Unlike the touch on his neck that had choked him to the ground, this touch had been gentle and it soothed him. After a time he had become accustomed to it and allowed it without alarm. It was something that had been new and now no longer was. Because of the pain in his leg and the great exhaustion of his body he lay down on the ground.

Inside the house Felipe got into his bed and pulled the quilt up for warmth.

They slept.

* * *

Each time the doctor checked on the wounded man he expected to find a body with the life expired, and each time he did not. It was no different this morning. Doctor Kountz lived in back of his office. The shingle out front explained the arrangement. There was no hospital for housing a person badly ill or near death like this Mendoza, and so he made do when he had to by placing the patient in the extra bedroom he kept ready.

Widowed a decade before, the pleasant existence so carefully built in Boston turned dull and tiresome—now this last adventure, on the edge of the advance across the land. He still tasted breakfast on his tongue—pancakes, made with fresh eggs and sweetened with sorghum syrup, the only sweetener available out here except for the occasional jar of honey from a grateful patient.

There was a little improvement in the wounded man, if that was possible. The drainage tube was still in place, left there after he'd laved the body cavity and sutured the incision. No point in replacing the stitch the Anderson woman had made in the intestine; it seemed to be holding well, and the vegetable fiber should be easily absorbed. He couldn't be certain he'd gotten out all the mess she'd slathered into the wound, but he had done his best. Imagine. And yet—no fever today.

He picked up the piece of lead he'd taken out of Mendoza.

So very close to the spinal cord. Perhaps too close. No doubt it had compressed nerves. It would be interesting to see if the man would be able to walk later. If he lived, of course.

The doctor was listening to the heartbeat when he felt a stirring under his stethoscope. Mendoza took in a deep breath. He opened his eyes and studied Kountz for a few moments.

"I thought angels was prettier."

"No, that's an old lie. They all look just like me."

Mendoza nodded, as if he understood, then slept again. Kountz finished with him and went down the street.

The sheriff glanced up from the papers on his desk when the door opened. He was at it early this morning, due in court in two hours and not enough time in his day to make room for all that needed doing.

"That Mendoza fellow's conscious, Ames."

"The Mexican? Supposed to die?"

"That's him, but he's not."

"Mexican?"

"Dead."

"Guess I better come talk to him. He say who shot him?"

"No, just that I'm not as pretty as he'd hoped, but I've heard that before."

Kountz stayed out in the front office, ready for patients, and Ames Bradberry went back alone. Mendoza looked asleep, but at the sound of Bradberry's heavy boots on the floor he opened his eyes.

"Howdy. I'm the county sheriff. Need to ask you a thing or two."

Mendoza nodded.

"How'd you get shot?"

The wounded man was weaker than he appeared. His voice was thin. "Man with a rifle, out on the prairie."

"Anybody you know?"

A shake of the head.

"How'd you end up at the Anderson place?"

"Don't know. Got on my horse, woke up here."

"You're not from around here, are you?"

"Did some work for Duncan."

"That Englishman up close to the fort?"

"Yes."

"I'll send somebody and let him know."

"No, don't." If that was not fear on the man's face it was close to it.

"Some reason you don't want him to know you're here?"

Kountz had been standing quietly in the doorway. "Ames, he's still plenty sick. I wish you'd wait til later for any more."

But Bradberry sensed something here. "You afraid of Duncan?"

Isidro shook his head and looked away.

"Come on Ames. Later, please."

"Okay, Doc, okay." He followed Kountz out with a quick study back at the patient. Something there, all right. More to it than the man had told.

CHAPTER 19

THE sheriff headed back to his office and met a couple walking the other direction, toward the cafe. He raised his hat.

"Morning Miss Clawson, James."

He allowed himself a private smile when they were past. Something interesting going on? He'd have to check the latest gossip.

James still felt surprised. He'd already been at work building shelves, making room for more merchandise, a little sweaty even in the morning cold. Sawing and hammering would do that to you. The last person he would've expected to see so early was Jezzie Clawson, but there she was, and a welcome sight, too.

"I am so bold today," she'd said, "as to ask your presence at the breakfast table."

He'd almost dropped the hammer he was holding, almost tripped over a board in his haste to straighten his clothing and sweep his hair back from his eyes. What was it she'd said?

"Breakfast?"

"Yes. Do you eat it?"

"I do. I certainly do." The understanding came to him that she had issued an invitation.

"Well?"

And so he'd washed his hands and run a wet comb through his hair and they had gone walking down the early street.

James had found no interest in women since the day Sarah had turned him down. It was because he had put everything into the belief that she would marry him. Ever since he'd come back from the fighting she had been his focus and his dream, even with the antics of her boy, the drinking and fighting. Then, to watch her marry Hub and make the home that James had thought would be his own; it had dulled his spirit for a long time, left him lonely and what was worse—wanting to stay that way. Like an old wounded bear licking his hurt in silence. If Hub hadn't come out here after cows, if there'd been more time to court her...but no, she had never loved James like that, and when he was honest with himself he understood that all the dreaming had been his own. Foolish man; but he had paid the price and was done with it now.

That must be true, because the pretty woman who sat at the table with him, who brushed the sawdust off his shirt sleeve, had lit a lamp inside him. His hot coffee tasted better than usual and the coming sun was brighter on the street outside.

When they finished the meal he headed back to the store alone. People were out now, a few men carrying headaches to the only saloon in town for the remedies on tap there. He himself had once chased off hangovers that way as a rebel soldier, but that was no way of life for a serious man. For that matter, the town would be better off without a saloon at all, but you might as well try wishing away the sun or the moon. In truth, they were lucky to have just one so far. There would be more.

Two riders went past him at a trot, as though they had purpose in front of them. They looked like master and servant. The master wore smooth, high-top boots up to his knees, pants that bloused out at the hip and a flat-brimmed planter's hat. His horse was a blooded racer, while the other man was an ordinary cowpoke on a narrow-chested gray probably roped out of the remuda before daylight. Both were strangers. They tied up in front of the sheriff's office.

Through the front window Ames Bradberry watched the two men dismount and head for his door. Court in an hour, Gus not in yet and now visitors. The dude in front carried a riding crop and removed his hat as he came inside. Bradberry stood up.

"Good morning, gentlemen."

"Sheriff?" You'd have to call the man short and thin. His mustache was like that, too, and his mouth cut across his face in the way you saw in people who had too much of everything. The guy behind him looked like a poorly-fed coon hound ashamed of something he'd just done.

He held out his hand. "Yes, sir. I'm Bradberry."

"William McGee, Sheriff. This man is one of my ranch hands, Peck Thomas. We've come to report two murders."

"Well, have a seat, then. What's happened?" He figured he already knew.

McGee turned the narrative over to Thomas and the sheriff found himself hoping Thomas was better with cattle than he was with words.

"See, sir, we was out checking cattle, you know counting and watching out for hurt ones and dead ones. The wolves get after 'em sometimes and cougars and there's a squatter at the edge of Mr. Mcgee's ranch, a free black that's fenced off a claim."

"It was you and two other men doing all that cattle counting?"

"Yes, sir, and they opened fire on us from over on his side of that blamed fence."

"Why?"

Thomas shrugged, reached for his Bull Durham, thought better of it, said, "We never give him no reason. Two of 'em was shootin' at us. The other waddies went down. They hit my horse, but I got away and went back to report it to Mr. McGee."

"You sure your friends are dead?"

"Oh, yeah, I know dead when I see it."

"I reckon this free black you're speaking of is Charlie Boone?"

McGee broke in. "That's correct. I checked the land records."

"Than you know Charlie ain't squatting on the land. He bought it. He owns it from heaven to hell."

"All right, then. My mistake."

"You're Walt's nephew?"

"That's right, and I have power of attorney in his affairs."

"How's Walt doing?"

"I doubt he could tell you what year it is, or what day. Otherwise..." he flipped a hand.

"So Charlie Boone killed off two of your men and then he cut a quarter-mile of fence to make it look like something besides what your Mr. Thomas just told me."

McGee raised his eyebrows. "I know nothing about the fence. You, Peck?"

"No sir. We never touched his fence."

"I'm short on time. Why don't we take a walk down to the funeral parlor?"

Five minutes later Peck Thomas took one look at the bodies and said, "Yeah, them's my pards. Dadgum shame they was shot down in cold blood thataway."

To the smiling undertaker in the dark suit McGee said,

"I'd appreciate it if you'd see to burying them in the nearest cemetery. I'll take care of the cost."

"Do you wish a full funeral service?"

"No, I won't be coming in for it. Just plant them. I'll let their families know, if we can find anyone."

Gus was at his desk when they returned. Bradberry said, "I have to make a court appearance. My deputy here will take your statements and I'll be back quick as I can. Stay around town and we'll talk some more."

When he returned at mid-morning Gus told him, "No, those men, they didn't stay and wait for you. The short one said tell you he'll be back some other day."

"Yeah, I expect he will."

CHAPTER 20

ROBERT Duncan rode the stallion twice around the pen, then at his nod the two ranch hands removed the barrier.

Elmo called after him, "You be careful now, Mr. Duncan." The Englishman smiled at that, well aware that Elmo would gladly watch him trampled under the animal's feet. No matter. Good, in fact, because it had never been affection he sought from the men who worked his spread. Fear and respect. That's what he insisted on.

And he had a pacer now. Just feel this one move. Limping a bit, yes, but otherwise smooth as a rocking chair. Once he taught the stallion to hold his head up and put a graceful arch in his neck, what a sight the two of them would make. He touched a spur to the dun's flank and drank the cold air, reining the mustang in a slow circle that would take them back to headquarters.

This was even better than he'd hoped—the wild creature that everyone had tried so hard to capture belonged to him. Had offered no resistance, had stood while saddle and bridle went on, while Robert mounted, and now followed the urging of rein and knee as if he'd always carried a rider—this rider. Letting him walk now. There seemed to be a bit of trouble with the left eye, and the limping was more pronounced, but that would clear up. Accidents happened when you trained an animal like this one. The mane and tail were trim now, the mane roached and stiff under the palm of Robert's hand, the tail no longer the black barbaric trail of a comet, but sheared back and rounded at the tip, high enough above the scrub to escape burrs and thorns. Elmo had done a good job on it. Perhaps he'd tell him so.

A stranger, cowhand by his looks, stood with the others watching, and he saw Estrella walking from the house to see him ride. Or to see the mustang's condition, more likely, after her ministrations of the previous day. Still a hundred yards away, he stopped the horse and dismounted. It might be prudent to tie a lead rope on this one, but he would not. They would see the complete submission he had accomplished.

Perfect. The stallion kept at his shoulder, following like a dog, and when he reached the small group of watchers he felt gratified by the looks on their faces.

Elmo said, "Hard to believe you trained him so fast, Mr. Duncan."

"He is limping," Estrella told him.

"Yes, yes, I know, but the leg will be fine. I won't ride him again for a few days."

Elmo again, "Man's here about a job."

Robert heard the exhalation of air through his wife's beautiful lips as she walked away.

"Won't you stay and watch, Estrella?" She didn't answer.

"Take the stallion, Elmo. In a stall, I think, until his leg is better."

And to the job seeker he said, "What is your name?"

The name wasn't important, of course, and he forgot it as soon as the man spoke it. The cowboy was well put together, looked strong enough, and Duncan gave him the choice.

"This will seem a bit strange to you, I suppose." They

always gave him full attention at this point. "I won't hire a man who won't fight. Do you fight?"

"I've had my share, I reckon." Funny, but they all said that, most often in the very same words.

"Boxing, I mean. In a ring. Bare knuckled."

"Well, no sir. I never done nothing like that."

"Are you willing?"

"I don't know. Who would I fight?" He was nervous now.

"Me."

"Reckon I don't understand."

"It's simple enough. I won't hire you unless you fight me. Gives me an opportunity to judge your mettle."

"And you'll give me a job if I have a go at you?"

"Guaranteed, if you beat me."

"And no job if I don't?"

"That depends on how well you conduct yourself losing."

The cowboy put his hands in his pockets and took a few steps, head down. He indicated the others standing around listening. "These men come to work that way?"

"Yes, every man who works here has fought me. As I say, I require it."

"How many's beat you?"

"None, so far. You could be the first."

"Okay, let's get it done."

The ring was a permanent structure in the back of the barn past the horse stalls. Posts hewn smooth by axe blade, ropes strung between them, and a dirt floor. Robert liked to wear high, lace-up shoes made for the purpose, and out of fairness, because horsemen always wore boots that would impair them in the contest, he provided three other sets in varying sizes for his opponents. A few minutes were required to get everything ready.

"The whitewash mark in the center of the ring is the scratch line," Duncan told the tall cowboy. "There will be no rounds, no stopping until one of us falls. The fallen fighter has half a minute to get up and get to the scratch mark. Vaughn Chambers, that fellow standing at ringside, will count aloud to thirty, serving as our clock. A knockout or failure to come to scratch ends the fight. Any questions?"

"No, sir, reckon not."

How good it felt to move this way, like a lion must feel closing in on its prey. Or a falcon. Robert extended his left hand in a jab, missed and crossed with his right, aiming at the man's jaw, almost hidden inside a ragged beard, trying to get it over with in a hurry. He failed to connect.

Then, before he could realize he'd been hit, Robert felt a sharp rip across his face and the ground came up fast, faster than it had ever happened before. No, it had never happened before.

Vaughn Chambers began his count at ringside. "One, two, three…"

Robert made it to his knees, then to his feet and found the scratch line. The cowboy was too dumb to come after him while he was groggy, but waited in a corner and Robert had time to get his head clear. It was a good blow, though. "You're a hard hitter," he said. The compliment was deserved.

They closed again and the cowboy hit him again, but it wasn't solid and he slipped it and put a fist in the man's stomach, doubled him over, and then brought an uppercut to the head that put the cowboy on the ground, hard. Robert backed away, confident the match was over. That punch had been perfect. His hand already felt swollen from the impact.

Chambers counted out the numbers, and at fifteen the fighter rose up and made scratch, then Robert was on him throwing blows from left and right, blood smearing both men, until the job seeker fell helpless into the ropes.

Robert didn't back away, but stayed on him, pounding at him with swollen fists until the men around the ring jumped inside and pulled him away. It was all done in silence, no one saying a word, as if this was something they had all seen before.

When he got his senses back, Robert said to Chambers, "Tell him there are no jobs available and send him away." Then, breathing hard and with blood on his fists, he walked bare-chested through the cold day toward his house.

CHAPTER 21

CHARLIE said, "Mighty good of you to come today, Hub. Don't know if me and Tom could get this done by ourselves."

All three had sweated through their shirts, even though the day was cool. They wore heavy leather gloves as protection from the barbs. Two rifles leaned against a tree not far from where they were working.

"Too bad them that done it can't be here to undo it," Hub said.

There was very little wire left over from the original fencing job, so they made do by splicing cut sections of wire together. Where the splices fell between posts the fence would be weaker, but it couldn't be helped.

Charlie said, "What we doin' could be all for nothin', you know. Wouldn't take them people but a few minutes to put this wire right back on the ground."

"Well, it's got to be up or you can't operate. And you and Tom can't stay out here watching fence all the time. Tell you the truth, I don't know what the answer is."

"There ain't but two good answers, and it's a choice of one or the other for us." He finished the splice and dropped the wire, stood to ease his back.

"What do you mean?"

"Rose is saying sell it and get out. She don't want to be

107

buryin' me or my boy, and she may be right about that. Ain't it just the way of this life, though? Man finally get things the way he wants it, and bang—somebody else come along , says no, sir, I'm here to tell you what you can have and what you can't have. It ain't right, and if we sell out like she says, it feels to me like we being cowards."

"Somewhere it says it's better to be a live dog than a dead lion."

"Why Hubbard Anderson, I believe you about to go to preachin'. So you think God, He's on Rose's side here? Wants me to be a live dog, stick my tail between my legs and go off and hide?"

"I'm pretty sure He don't want you bein' a dead lion."

"How about a live lion? I like that idea best."

"Yeah, I do, too. What's the other one?"

"Other what?"

"You said there was just two answers. What's the other one?"

"I can take a ride up that way and have a talk with them McGee folks. See if we can't reach some sort of understanding."

"Charlie, I can't even tell you how bad of an idea that is."

"What's so bad about it? What could happen?"

They heard the creak of saddle leather first, then the pop of a tree limb pushed forward and released, then a familiar voice.

"Don't shoot, men! It's Ames Bradberry!" He was approaching from inside Charlie's property, so he had come from the house and gotten directions from Rosabelle how to find them. There was a smile on the sheriff's face, lifting that broad mustache of his, so he was saying it in fun, but Hub didn't feel like it was all that funny just then. He'd already started for his rifle when Bradberry had called out.

The big man rode up and sat his horse, looking down on them. "Guess this's that wire you cut. Where'd you two stand to ambush them poor fellers?" He was still smiling, so this must still be funny.

Charlie said, "Ambush? Them poor fellers of yours was lined up in the timber right over yonder waiting on us, and they come out in a charge, firing their guns at us. Me and Tom ran back thataway, into the cedar."

"Don't pay me no mind, Charlie, I'm just hoorawin' you. No, that one that got away came into town with his boss and they say you ambushed 'em for no reason. You and that cold-blooded boy, Tom." He grinned at Tom and Tom grinned back at him.

Hub said, "I take it you don't believe what they told you."

"Not one word."

"But you don't have no proof one way or the other." Charlie.

"It's why I come out today, wanted to see where it happened." He got down off his horse and Charlie and Tom took him through the incident step by step.

He said, "It's easy enough to see the men were sent out here to do it, and it was that little short guy from Mississippi that did the sending. He's brought them old ideas with him and resents a free black sharing his country."

"That would be me," Charlie said.

"It would. As you probably know, the state's made it so all the freed slaves trying to find a way to live can't homestead land like white folks can. They can't live on it and prove it up. That keeps 'em dependent on whites for someplace they can work for wages or on shares. But Charlie, here, has gone way around and come up on the other side, as you might say. He had some money and bought his land. And fenced it. And is making a good life for his family. So, naturally, everybody is mad about it. Probably nothing would ever have come of their mad, but this little Mississipi sugar ant has done what nobody else around here would have, and I think the fat's in the fire."

Hub said, "There's got to be a way to stop it. It ain't right Charlie's got to work scared of what they'll do to him and his family. And it sure ain't right for him to sell out and leave."

"No, and I plan on addressing the problem. I'm heading out to McGee's ranch in the morning. Since Ben knows Walt McGee, I've asked him to go with me. And I'd like you along, too, Hub, if you can go. It'll help to show that Charlie's got friends that will stand up for him."

"I can go. We'll finish here by dark."

"Good. Can you meet us at Ben's about sunup?"

"I'll be there."

Charlie stepped up. "What about me, Sheriff? I got a right to be there and hear what's said about me."

"This ain't about rights just now. You have friends, Charlie, trying to keep you healthy. I suggest you sit still for a while and allow us to do it."

CHAPTER 22

HUB caught and penned the line-back gelding in the corral along with the mare before he went in the house to eat Sarah's supper, finishing the day's work in the dark with just enough moonlight that he could see his way.

"I thought you'd want to travel to Ben's with me and stay til I come back," he told her around a mouthful of beef.

"That will be fine," she said, "if you get me back at an early hour. I don't want to come home in the dark with the chores in front of me."

They were up long before dawn, Marie asleep on her father's shoulder, wrapped in a warm blanket, the two horses walking single-file to the Bent-T down the old Fort McKavett road. Sarah was ahead on the gelding. She wore the blue scarf he'd bought in town. Hub called out—"I forgot to tell you, the sheriff says that fellow you doctored is alive and awake. Everybody's surprised."

"No more than me," she said.

There were three figures on the porch, visible by the light of the just-rising sun. Wood smoke brushed across them, carried off the chimney by a tender downdraft of wind. Ben told them, "John, here, thought he'd go with us, but the sheriff thinks that's one too many."

Bradberry said, "I don't want to give the appearance that we've come looking for a fight."

Sarah hugged her tall son and carried the baby into the house behind him. She said, "This is nice, Johnny. We can have a long talk."

The three men, Hub, Ben, and Ames Bradberry, began their long ride.

They pushed ahead without a pause and came in sight of the ranch headquarters in the middle of the morning, sun warming things, lines of salty sweat forming on the shoulders of their horses. Been a while since we've had rain, Hub thought. Hope we're not going to have a drought. The north Llano river kept his cattle, as well as Ben's and Charlie Boone's supplied with water, but it was a shallow river and he'd heard tales of dry times that had shut it down to a few trickles.

Ben Turner said, "Place has changed some since I seen it last." The approach to the house was paved with decomposed pink granite that reminded Hub of the mesa where he'd caught the stallion. Somebody had hauled wagon loads of it here and used it to pretty effect. The horses' hoofs crunched in it. Small trees, no more than five or six feet high, had been planted at intervals. The time would come when a rider would be shaded here. "What are they?" Ben asked nobody in particular. "Cottonwoods?"

"Yeah," from the sheriff. It looked like the barn had been torn down and at a new site farther from the house men moved around, lifting boards and climbing ladders. The faint sound of hammers reached them.

A woman of middle age, looking like she had been picked up and moved here from some southern cotton plantation, print scarf wrapped around her head, white dress and a black apron that matched her skin, opened the door when they knocked. They'd already discussed among themselves the way that seemed best.

Bradberry said, "We've come to visit Walt. Is he at home?"

"Yes, sir, he is, but..."

"Well, we know he's sick, but we're old friends of his."

"I ought to ask Mister William first."

"Where is he?"

"Down yonder where they buildin', I think."

"Just save us all that trouble, why don't you. He took his badge out of the shirt pocket where he'd put it a few minutes ago, showed it to her. "I'm the county sheriff, and I want to see Walt."

She looked at the badge and then at Bradberry and then back at the badge. "All right, Sheriff, y'all can come on in, I guess."

CHAPTER 23

IT was an old house, expanded over many years from the original log cabin, rooms added, halls added to reach the rooms. Once full, as Ben remembered it, of people and conversation. There'd been a funeral service for Walt's wife in one of the rooms long before the war, dead of some unnamed disease, then the boy who went off in uniform and never returned, the daughter married now and living on the east coast.

A chamber pot was hidden under the bed, but the room held its odor. The old man sat in a rocking chair, dressed as though he might soon mount a cow pony and ride off to see about his stock. His skin was dry and close about his skull, his eyes like marbles floating in milk, one long tooth showing between his parted lips. He watched them come through the door into the room.

"Walt? It's Ben Turner."

The old man gathered himself as if to rise, then seemed to give up the idea. His voice had no force at all behind it. "Come in, Ben. Have a seat." He watched the three of them as they pulled up wooden chairs in a tight semicircle.

"Can I offer you gentlemen some refreshment?" The woman waited in the open doorway. When they all shook their heads she closed the door.

"This here's my son-in-law, Hubbard Anderson, and I think you know Ames Bradberry."

McGee nodded. "Good day, Sheriff."

Bradberry said, "Mr. McGee, I know your nephew has power of attorney in regards to your ranch. What I want to hear from you is whether it's about your ability to get around or because you have grown...forgetful, let's say."

McGee found that funny, exposed his near toothless gums in a grin and scratched at his forehead. "Gone loco—that's what you mean, ain't it?"

Bradberry left off comment and waited.

"My brother lost everything he owned out there in Mississippi. Without his slaves he couldn't...anyhow, he lost his land to creditors. He sent his boy, William, to me. I guess you've met him. No prospects for him there, so I offered to help him. I turned it over to him to run, yeah. Seems like my girl has forgot the place. But it ain't on account of my mind. It's these old legs that won't carry me no more."

Bradberry said, "Your nephew infers it is your mind, the reason for the changeover."

"Wouldn't put it past him. Don't know as it makes no difference, anyhow. I'll be headin' for the barn pretty soon now."

Ben said, "Well, don't forget they've moved it."

McGee laughed and rubbed his hand over his face and head again.

Bradberry said, "I don't reckon it was you sent three men to cut fence a few days ago."

"I hate bob wire. Worst thing ever invented."

"It ain't a favorite of mine, either, but I wouldn't cut what belonged to another man."

"You saying I done that? No, that's wrong. I ain't knowed nothing about it."

"I didn't think so, but I needed to ask you. And I need to ask your nephew while I'm out here."

"Ask his nephew what?" The door swung open as the sheriff talked, and William McGee stood there, dressed much as he had been in town, including the riding crop.

"Details that concern your complaint. Can we go somewhere else to talk? I believe your uncle is tired."

William took them into a parlor filled with good furniture. It had been cleaned, but still contained the faint smell of dust and mold. The glass panes in the room's one window had been wiped spotless outside and inside, letting in unimpeded sunlight. White, starched curtains hung on either side of it. When Hub sat down in the overstuffed chair he wondered if he'd ever be able to get out of it.

William called for coffee, and after the maid brought it Ames Bradberry took a sip from his cup and said, "I've been out to the Boone place where all that business happened, and it looks to me like what you told me don't stand up."

"What?" William leaned forward. "You're saying my man lied?"

Bradberry didn't address the question straight on. "I used to scout for the army and I read sign pretty good, Mr. McGee. What I read backed up Charlie's story, not yours."

"Why are these two men here?" He asked the sheriff, pointing to Ben and then Hub with his riding crop, still leaning forward in the chair.

"Long ride out here. I invited them along for company."

William sat back and tapped his knee with the crop. "What I told you about the incident was what Peck Thomas related to me. I believed it to be true then, and I still do."

"I wonder, could we include Peck in out conversation? Maybe he could clear up my doubts."

"Sorry, he's quit and gone somewhere north. It bothered him, seeing his friends killed."

"Well sir, with your only witness gone and with what the sign out there indicates to me, I don't see how I can bring charges against Charlie Boone. Is that what you expect me to do?"

"Either that, or I'll see to it that a grand jury hears the matter."

"No, we're not sending it to no grand jury of white men who got it in for Boone anyhow. Wouldn't be hard to get him indicted, and I know he didn't do it. Just like you know it, if I'm not mistaken." He stared hard at William. Ben and Hub kept quiet.

A smile came and went on the small man's face. "Your working premise, then, is that I sent them after Boone."

"Correct."

"I've never before known a lawman to side with coloreds against his own people."

Bradberry didn't react. McGee sat back in his chair. The look on his face reminded Hub of a small boy who's done something naughty and is proud of it.

When the sheriff stood, Ben and Hub followed suit. "That's not much of an insult out here. What I work for is the fair application of the law, black or white. What I see is a Mississippi planter who resents a black man owning property that blocks him from a mile of the Llano river." McGee also left his chair as though he was about to reply, but Bradberry stopped him. "Don't bother denying it. You figure to run right over him and have your way. Well, you won't get my help to do it. These men's neither. Charlie's got friends, and I brought these two along to show you that. So, to the question you asked a while back, there's your true answer why they're with me."

"I have nothing more to say to you, Sheriff. Good day." He walked from the room and left them standing there.

They heard him yell out, "Ivy!"

A few seconds later she appeared at the door. "I'll show you gentlemen out, if you please."

Ben said, "I'd like to say goodbye to Walt."

"He's in the bed asleep, sir. But I'll be sure to tell him for you when he wakes up." They followed her wide figure down a dark hall to the bright day outside.

CHAPTER 24

GUSTAVE Meyer sat at his desk watching the street through the front window. He didn't know when Sheriff Bradberry would be back in town, probably not before dark, maybe not til morning. The jail cells were empty. There'd been no trouble.No big trouble, anyhow, just a man who wouldn't pay for his drink in the saloon—always something going on over there. Gus felt nervous when his boss was away. He'd never meant to be a deputy sheriff, had always been a farmer like his father before him, on the outskirts of Berlin. The hope of free land had lured him, as it had many German immigrants, to America, then to Texas, and confusion had set in. The state was so big it was hard to decide where to settle.

Many Germans had come out here to the wilder lands on the frontier, but these lands were not ideal for farming. The soil was alkaline and thin, and rain undependable. This country was better used in raising cattle, maybe sheep. He could move south, toward the ocean, or even to the eastern side of the state and find better soil for the growing of crops. Trouble was, he had loved it here from the first time he had seen it—the hills and the pretty water. A while back he had no longer been sure he could leave and Bradberry had put a sign in his window, DEPUTY WANTED, and Gus had asked for the job.

The town and the countryside around it seemed to change on a daily basis. Why, this had been the western frontier only yesterday it seemed to him, but the frontier had quickly moved on past them and sort of vanished like fog in sunshine, without an edge to it, leaving behind a normal life to be lived day to day, like anywhere else. The street was always busy, people riding into town and out of town, on what business he could only guess. Like the tall cowboy on the rangy, tired sorrel passing now at a slow walk. The man's hat was pulled down on his ears against the cold afternoon, his rough jacket buttoned to the chin. Like all the other riders in the street, this one went on past the window and out of sight.

It had been many months, and Jezzie didn't recognize the new customer at first. His face had changed some, hollowed out, like he hadn't had enough to eat, shrunken from the cold wind outside, his beard ragged and in need of scissors.

"Howdy, Jezzie." One of his eyes looked bruised.

"You been in a fight?"

He grinned, and for a second his old self shone in his face. "Kind of. I was lookin' for a job west of here and the man wanted me to fight him for it. I lost."

"That can't be right. My brother doesn't lose fights."

"Oh, well, there was rules, a ring and everything. It was the rules, I expect, that whipped me."

"Or maybe you haven't had a good meal in a month."

"That too, maybe."

"How'd you find me?"

He glanced around the room. "I went looking in 'Frisco. One of your old pals told me you hauled a bunch of clothes to Texas, to be a merchant lady. When I didn't find you in El Paso or San Antonio I figured this is where you'd be.

"I guess it's money you want."

"No, Jez, you're wrong there. Anyway, I got a job. No, first off I just wanted out of California, then I wanted to know where you'd gone off to. I was always more sentimental than you, even when we was little kids."

"You know, Raiford, either one of us could still be hung for that business when we left here."

He said, "Town's changed. I can't even figure out where it was that Juanito got gunned off his horse."

"The building is gone. That whole bunch, the police troop, was disbanded. A friend of yours killed the captain. He was in here the other day, said give you his regards."

"I didn't know I had one of them—a friend."

"Hubbard Anderson? Ranches somewhere west of town. He said you saved his life."

It took a second. "Why, I believe I did. A bull got after him. I recall it now."

"Would he know it was us stole the money?"

"I can't say. I never saw him again after I took him to a ranch house."

She drew the curtains on the only window and flipped the closed sign into view. "Let's go down the street and have a good supper."

They took their time over the food. Few customers were in the cafe that time of day, just before most businesses closed, and they had a corner table to themselves. She finished long before her brother, who seemed to have the appetite of two men. Sipping at the cup of cooling coffee she said, "Maybe you ought to go back to Missouri."

"I told you, I got a job. Anyway, I don't want to go back there. I imagine the family's all dead by now, and I will be, too, if I show my face again."

"Well, I admit it would feel nice to have you living somewhere close, but you be careful around here. The sheriff's Ames Bradberry, and he's nobody to fool with."

"You needn't worry, Jez. I'll behave and let you be respectable, if that's what you're after." He bit on the word respectable like it was a rock hidden in his beans.

"What's wrong with that, Raif? I tell you, I'm worn out with schemes and lies and dodges. What I want more than anything else is to settle down someplace—here, maybe—and get so respectable I stink. I'm tired of that old life. Don't want any more of it."

He ate the last bite of his second beefsteak, chewed it slowly as he looked at her with understanding eyes. "You won't get no argument from me on that account, Jezzie. Does that little store of yours make you a living?"

"It does all right. I don't look to haul in a fortune like I used to. Yeah, I do all right. But you never said what happened to you out in California. I thought you had bought out a claim that would make you some money."

"Oh, I sold it. Turned out I liked to talk about gold mining, and I liked to think about it, but I didn't like the actual work. After I sold it I tried to run up my stake in one or two poker games."

"And lost it all."

"Seems like I did, yes."

They were silent for a few seconds. A clatter of dishes sounded from somewhere behind the counter. She said, "I thought when we rode out with all that money we'd be set for life. I'm surprised it didn't pan out that way."

"And we would've been, except we were ignorant Missouri hillbillies, Jezzie. You picked a crook to partner with in that danged saloon, and I couldn't keep away from poker tables. There you have the story."

"Maybe so, but the story changes right here and now." The day was about finished. Long shadows stretched across the street outside. "You plan to stay in town tonight?"

"You know me. I don't exactly plan."

"I have a room in a boarding house, but I can't keep you there. Probably a room over the saloon if you don't mind piano music most of the night. And your horse. There's a livery stable now. I'll loan you enough to see you through."

"I'd be obliged, Jezzie, if it won't squeeze you too bad."

"What about that job you mentioned?"

"It starts in a day or two. I signed on with a rancher a few miles north, name of McGee. I'm his new regulator."

CHAPTER 25

HUB fed the horses while Sarah took care of the chickens. It wasn't quite dark, but she was a little put out anyway at the lateness of the day. The Jersey cow had come up from pasture and stood waiting a turn at feed and milking. Marie was asleep in the house, but she'd soon be awake and wanting a feeding of her own. Some days were just too hard. She heard Hub rinsing out the milk bucket and called to him.

"I'll do that in just a minute."

"No, you go on in the house. I don't mind."

She'd been a little mad at him about his tardiness, knowing all the while he couldn't help it. The hens were in their coop feeding on grain, and she closed the door against coyotes and foxes and other lovers of chicken meat and walked past Hub as he readied the milk stool. She shoved the stool aside and put her arms around him, remembering the time he had proposed to her before the cattle drive. How he had stood there with hat in hand and fear on his face, and how she'd kissed him then as she kissed him now, leaving his eyes wide and his face alight.

"I love you, Hubbard Anderson."

"And I don't mind that a bit, Sarah."

"You could be a little more romantic, you know."

"I won't be long at the milking, girl, and you better watch out. You'll get all the romantic you can use."

She laughed and slapped at his arm and went in the house feeling happy, feeling safe.

The mare never grazed far from the house and was almost always within calling distance at morning. He only penned her at night if early work was necessary. The other two, the mule and gelding, he left hobbled now, not that they were apt to run off, but he couldn't bring himself to trust them since they'd gone with the wild stallion so willingly. Maybe Charlie was right about the wire—fence off your property and simplify things. But what could be more out of place than sharp steel barbs hanging on fences all over this open country? It was certain to come, whether he agreed with it or not, and they would all begin living inside wire boxes. But not yet.

He wandered into the pasture and whistled for her and in two or three minutes she appeared around a live oak five hundred yards away. He'd been riding her every day lately and wanted to give her some corn. The morning wasn't freezing, but it was cold enough to numb his fingers. A gray cloud rose from the chimney behind him, and he smelled the smoky flavor of it in the air. The dun followed the mare, and he appeared to have lost his hobbles. Then the mule. And another dun. One of the duns was hobbled, one walked free.

That couldn't be the stallion. Duncan had him. But there he was, trotting up as though it happened this way every day. Hub wished for his pistol, but it was in the house, nothing in his hand but a halter. The stallion didn't look wild now, his mane and tail trimmed like any well-kept horse, but it was him, all right. Even at this distance Hub could see the dark wound on his neck where the Mendoza fellow had shot him. A hundred yards away the animal stopped and stood watching the mare walk up and wait for the halter.

So he got away somehow. But you'd expect him to head back to his own country, not come all these miles east. Still, he didn't have a manada now and his instinct would be to gather mares and other followers, and he'd already been on a raid here once. He came for the mare again. That must be it. But he didn't take her. Maybe he couldn't take her. He had been beaten, that much was obvious, still limping on a foreleg. So he came up in the middle of the night and said to the mare, come with me, and she said, don't believe so. And he wasn't strong enough to insist.

Hub wasn't about to approach the stallion on foot. He remembered the click of teeth the day they captured him on the mesa. He slipped the halter on the mare's head and with a smooth leap put himself on her back and used the halter rope to guide her. At first the mustang shied back, nickering deep in his throat, eyes showing white. Hub talked to him, brought the mare in close again. And then a second time. For her part, she never hesitated, had lost her early fear of the wild one. Nobody was there to talk it over with, so Hub talked to the mare.

"He could come for my leg, maybe pull me off. I might ought to get away from him, you think?" He nudged her with a knee and she stepped even closer, close enough for Hub to reach out and touch the muscular neck. His hand trembled a little as he did it. "I guess you could swing around and kick me a mile if you was a mind to."

But there was no kick, no aggressive charge. Hub stroked the stallion, felt muscles move under his fingers, and surveyed the damage, the scabs over wounds that were beginning to heal.

"Somebody put a bad whipping on you, old friend. Reckon I can guess who it was."

Down the mustang's chest and left shoulder there was partially dried blood, a lot of it, but there was no fresh wound on the horse so it had come from something or somebody else.

"You've had a long night. Well, come on, let's get you some corn and water." He slid off the mare and led her toward the corral. He didn't look back until they were almost there. The stallion had followed along, was back a few paces behind them. Hub walked her inside and tied the halter rope to the trough then brought a sack of corn out of the barn, ignoring the weary stranger who stood all the while outside the corral, watching. He filled the trough, then walked through the barn and back to the house.

"Sarah, come see." Just his head was inside the door.

She looked away from the dishpan. "See what?" Her heart tripped a little at the sound of excitement in his voice.

"Come on, hurry."

She peeked in at Marie as she dried her hands on a towel and followed Hub outside.

He kept his voice low, nearly a whisper. "That stallion showed up this morning."

"But how on earth...?"

"I don't know. Got away from Duncan somehow, bloodied up real good like he's been fighting." They went through the barn to the back where he'd left the door open to the corral. She held onto his arm when he started through the door.

"Is he dangerous?" Still whispering.

"I don't think so. Stay behind me."

Both animals stood at the feed trough. The mare paid them no mind, but the stallion shied away as they emerged from inside the building. Hub and Sarah waited quietly and in a couple of minutes he took a tentative step toward the trough, then another, and made his way to the corn again.

"Poor fellow," Sarah said, "He's had a beating." She continued to stare at the mustang and then began a slow walk toward him.

"Wait, Sarah."

But she didn't wait. She ignored Hub's caution and walked between the mare and the visitor, bent down and got a handful of grain, offered it to him. Hub had come up beside her, fearful of what could happen. But it was all right. The stallion took her offer, his long red tongue raking her hand clean.

"He's beautiful. I thought he'd be larger."

"No, these Spanish ponies don't get very big, but they can run bigger horses into the ground."

"Look where they shot him."

"He's lucky it didn't kill him. That's what usually happens. Mendoza must be a good shot."

"What happens now?

He shrugged. "Hard to say. No brand on him, I guess Duncan's got no legal right to him. But from what I saw the other day, they'll be on this boy's trail. Probably are right now. Duncan's a strange one. He'll have him back or kill him, I expect."

"We can hide him."

"How'd you go about hiding a horse, Sarah?"

"In the barn, if he'd stay there. Would he?"

"I don't know, but I don't intend playing that game. No, he's free to come and go and I'll leave it at that."

"Then what will happen if Duncan shows up?"

"Hard to say." He didn't meet her eyes.

"You're worrying me, Hub. Are you looking to fight him? I won't have you hurt or killed over this horse." It might have been a twirl of smoke from the chimney that wet her eyes.

"Let's go in the house." He led her by the hand back through the barn and into their kitchen where a fire had burned for hours. It had warmed the wood of the walls, the floor they stood on, filled the room with the sweet scent of its burning. He flexed his stiff fingers in the sudden warmth.

"I wish things would stay simple. We got any more coffee?"

She poured a cup for him.

He said, "That danged stud out there is a whole lot more trouble than he's worth. Could be the blood on him is Duncan's. Maybe the Englishman hit him one time too many and got what was coming to him."

"He was gentle around us."

"We ain't harmed him, though, and he's tuckered out to boot, from traveling. And from mistreatment."

The sharp crack of a rifle sounded outside.

"I guess they've killed him." Hub put down his cup, strapped on his gunbelt, got his rifle from where it leaned in a corner, handed it to Sarah and said, "Stay here."

CHAPTER 26

I T was Duncan, all right, with a handful of riders. Three men were down on foot a few hundred yards away, the others in a tight turn around them. Hub found the mare alone. No time to saddle up. He slid onto her back and left the corral at a trot. He recognized Robert Duncan by his puffy shirt and his bearing in the saddle. The wind was cold and dry in Hub's nose and his heart struggled with rage and indecision. A horse was on the ground, and it was a dun with a line down his back. The wild stallion didn't have a line on him. Duncan dismounted, still holding the rifle, did a double-take when he recognized Hub.

The line-back dun had been contrary, but still there was regret in seeing him like that, head back, eyes open and dull, blood emptying from the wound in his side. No attempt to crease an animal this time.

One of the riders, a man he had never seen before, said, "We tracked a mustang here, mister. Thought it was this one."

Hub stared at him, unable to speak, not trusting his voice. This was what loving and marrying did to you, then. He could still see the tears in Sarah's eyes this morning, hear her words, *I won't have you hurt or killed.* He thought his way through the knowledge that in order to be a husband a man gives up part of manhood. Here was Duncan in front of him again, and already he'd backed off once, let it go when he ought to've forced the issue. Now it was all to do again, backing out of trouble, and he wasn't sure he could, because the black rage filled his head.

He looked at Duncan. "Was it you shot my horse?"

"Afraid so. My apologies." There was none of the arrogance on the man's face that Hub remembered so well from their last meeting. He felt his shoulders sag, looked away. One of the cowboys came closer, the one called Elmo, his face grimed with trail dust. Exhaustion covered him like a second set of clothes.

"We didn't know whose place we was on, mister. Thought your dun was that stallion. We trailed him most of the night."

"What's the hurry? You could catch him anytime."

"You remember Mr. Duncan's black stallion? Well, that dun got out of his stall and went in the pasture and fought the black. Killed him. It was their screams woke everybody up and he was lit out by the time we got there."

Duncan remounted, one hand on the sadddle horn, the other holding the rifle he'd used to shoot the gelding. He said to Hub in a tired voice, "I'm sorry for this. I'll see that you're paid for the loss." He urged his horse away and the others followed.

Hub watched them go and held back his words and actions, stilled the voices and anger as best he could.

Through the window Sarah watched him ride in, the others disappear from sight. The fear in her ebbed and her breathing became normal. She put away the rifle she'd been holding, not sure what use she was supposed to put it to, grateful it wasn't needed. Hub never came in the house.

In a little while she heard the sound of the axe from the wood shed. He was splitting firewood. She walked out and stood behind him, out of the axe's way as it fell over and over again on the oak logs, the smell of fresh-cut wood in the cold air.

"They shot the dun," she said.

He ignored her statement, kept on splitting logs.

"They thought he was the stallion."

He said nothing.

"Are you mad at me, Hub? Have I done something to make you mad?" Still nothing from him. In the house Marie began crying. Nursing time again. She left the wood shed and walked to the back door, the axe coming down on the chopping block as regular as the pendulum of a clock. She glanced once at her husband, brushed an oak chip off the sleeve of her dress and went inside.

* * *

"Then you must leave here, there's no choice! Only God knows what Robert will do when he learns it was you."

Felipe's eyes were downcast, the food in front of him untouched. What she said was true, of course, but he needed her forgiveness more than her help. "I had to do it."

"Yes, I know you felt the pain of that stallion." Her voice had become flat. Concern was pointless. There was no way to make things in this house all right again, though she had wanted that—wanted her brother back again, wanted her husband to love her as he once had, cease treating her as though he owned her like he owned the animals on the range. It was not so much to want, but now it was finished. How could she not have guessed what Felipe would do?

"But it was not just the pain, you see. It was something else hard to describe—a blackness like the bottom of a well, an echo of nothing, the echo of an echo and blackness and it came from the poor horse like a strong wind until I couldn't bear it."

"Robert may try to kill you when he finds out. Probably he

knows it already. I have to take you somewhere safe, but where that place is, I don't know. Eat now. I'll saddle a horse and we'll leave before they get back. All the men are with Robert, so nobody will stop us, and nobody will know where we go."

An hour later they were headed east on the Fort McKavett road, the idea in her head that she would take him to Junction City. To the sheriff? A doctor? Maybe to a church. Anyone, anything, was better than leaving him to the anger of her husband. Felipe walked beside her pony, barefoot, in the rough trousers Isidro had brought him in wearing, and a white shirt she had sewed for him. She had cut his hair shorter, but it still hung long on his neck. He had insisted she leave it like that. And he wore no hat. They met no one on the road, which was good, so that none could give witness to their passage.

She had seldom been to Junction City and was uncertain how far it was from their ranch, how long it might take to reach it, was glad of the distance between, since distance might be a friend in keeping her brother and Robert Duncan apart until the fearful feelings could settle. They traveled in silence, Felipe keeping pace with her pony's gentle gait. Hours passed and the sun began settling behind her, the shadows in front growing longer, a chill in the air now. For the first time she realized she would be too far from home to return today. *Or did I know that all along?* This would only make more trouble.

Felipe spoke so faintly that at first she didn't hear him. He had stopped and was looking around into the trees. "Wait." This time she heard and reined the gray pony to a halt.

"What is it?"

"Him."

"Him? Do you mean Robert?"

"No, the stallion."

"What are you talking about, Felipe? Did you hear something?"

"I hear his heart beating."

CHAPTER 27

THIS filled her with great dread, because now she knew her brother was becoming crazy again and all her efforts to save him were no good. "You don't hear his heart, Felipe. Please, that you not be like this."

He began to walk away. She slapped the reins against her mount's neck and followed. "Where are you going?"

"The horse isn't far away. I don't know how to make you believe it, Estrella, but I know he's here, and he's afraid." Ahead of them a buggy road cut away northward into the woods, faint ruts rarely traveled, but leading somewhere.

"Come away, Felipe. We have to reach town before dark."

He didn't answer, but picked up his pace so that she had to urge the gray into a trot to keep up. The faint road was narrow, full of the odors of cedar oil and acorns. Limbs bare of their leaves brushed against her as she rode along it, fearful that her brother would leave her behind. Nothing restrained him, after all, and if he ran into the woods she could never find him again. Perhaps that's how this would end.

Somewhere ahead a sound began to make itself heard, dull and distant in the beginning, then sharper, steady. The sound of an axe? Movement beside the trail, a few cattle irritated at their passage. Estrella half expected, half feared seeing the dun pony at every bend in the trail. Felipe kept on.

The house was a surprise, looked to be waiting for them as

they came out of the timber, with more open ranch land behind it, rolling to the north. A cloud of buzzards circled something out there. A larger building, a barn, she decided, rose near the house, and the sound of the axe was clear now. Felipe would have veered around it all and continued, but she stopped him by spurring the gray forward and blocking her brother's way.

"Wait. Somebody lives here, we can't just go fumbling around after a horse."

"But he's not far. I need to go and find him." He sounded frantic and looked near tears. Estrella felt a little afraid of him at that moment. There was smoke from the chimney, someone probably inside, but she rode around back of the house to find the wood chopper and saw him in front of his shed, splitting the short logs that he retrieved, one after another, from inside it.

Hub caught their movement from the corner of his eye and lowered the axe. He saw a beautiful woman astride a gray pony, and walking behind her the man who believed he was a horse. He blinked his eyes, hoping they would be gone, nothing but imagination, but they remained there. He wiped a hand across his face and felt the grit of bark and wood chip, and realized the day was almost over, with the chores not done. Where was Sarah? Fled from his anger, probably, hiding from him inside with Marie, waiting out the storm that had come on him. He looked out at where the dun gelding lay dead beneath the circling black birds.

"Good afternoon. I'm Estrella Duncan, and this is my brother, Felipe."

Hub wiped his eyes again, made an effort to escape the reverie he'd been in for hours, felt the stiffness in his hands and fingers, walked on unsure feet toward them and said,

"Afternoon, ma'am. I'm Hubbard Anderson. Let me help you down. You folks look tired."

She dismounted, touched his offered hand briefly for balance, smoothed her clothing. She wore pants like a man, but it did not diminish the dark beauty that seemed to precede her as wind precedes the dark rain cloud. Her brother looked poised to run.

"Why don't y'all come in the house." His mind seemed thick and unresponsive, slow to understand. This was Robert Duncan's wife, but why had she come here? And the man—if he took off running they'd never catch him, yet there was no rope on him as Mendoza had used.

"Hub?" It was Sarah's voice. She'd heard the axe stop.

Explanations were quick, with Felipe anxious to continue, and a few minutes later Hub followed the man eastward along the edge of timber that skirted the cleared pasture. He carried a coiled lasso in his hand and wished he'd taken time to exchange moccasins for the boots he wore. His legs and feet were stiff and clumsy after all the hours he'd stood at the chopping block, and the man in front of him seemed as strong and swift as one of the young steers grazing nearby. Where would this business end? Felipe didn't sound crazy, and he seemed certain the stallion was out here. Hub had figured the horse gone back to the mesa, but of course with his mares scattered he'd be alone out there with nobody to boss around. Still, it was preposterous to think Felipe heard the animal's heartbeat, that he felt what the stallion felt, but the woman would have come if Hub hadn't—it seemed she found belief difficult in the things Felipe told them, and yet allowed him to express himself even in ways that made no sense.

Something hard contacted a rock in front of them. In a patch of shadow a darker shadow moved and there came the low, throaty rumble of recognition, answered in like manner by the brother. The stallion didn't come forward, but allowed them to approach and allowed the hand of Felipe to stroke his neck.

"You won't need the rope," came Felipe's voice. "He'll follow us back."

"And that's what happened," Hub told the women an hour later, after they'd walked him in and put out feed for the horses, including the one that had carried Mendoza , and the mule that had wandered up looking unsure, glancing back at the buzzards. The mule wasn't used to people and Hub figured she'd gone into hiding after the shooting and general commotion of the morning.

"You're sure he won't steal them all tonight?" Sarah's voice was cool. She'd had no chance to be alone with him since the rebuff at the wood shed. He found it difficult to remember why he'd treated her so badly, knew he was in the wrong and looked for a chance to tell her so.

"I hobbled ours, and Mendoza's gelding, too. I'm leaving the stallion loose, and won't mind a bit if he's gone when morning comes."

He heard a sharp intake of breath from Estrella Duncan. She was staring at him with questioning eyes.

CHAPTER 28

H E enjoyed the company of women as much as the next man, he supposed, but it was past time he got back to working his cattle. And now here he was on another errand that could lead to more trouble. Sarah had been all right this morning, willing to listen to his regret even though he'd offered not much of an explanation for his behavior. She'd made the brother and sister pallets near the fireplace, which was where Estrella had insisted on sleeping though they'd offered her their bed. Felipe seemed able to sleep anywhere, as if you could hang him by the door like a parasol or a rifle and find him ready and awake at morning.

The stallion had gone nowhere in the night. It looked like he'd decided to stay though Hub offered him every encouragement to go. They'd left Felipe back at the house where he spent his time talking to the animal, rubbing the injured skin with tender hands. Hub had at first declined to accompany the woman, but a sharp look from Sarah had caused him to rethink his answer, and so here he was again a couple of miles from Junction City after a silent ride, both of them occupied with their own thoughts. Estrella spoke.

"He was like that all his life."

"Pardon?" Hub rode over closer.

"Felipe. When he was little he talked to the dogs and cats."

She laughed. "The chickens, too. Now, it's just horses. Do you think I have to put him away somewhere?"

"Why, no, he seems harmless, I don't see why you ought to." He thought about the young man for a moment. "Hard to explain how he knew the mustang was out there, though. I can't figure it out."

"Well, no one can. But somehow he has that gift. That curse."

"Ask this doctor about it. Maybe he'll have an idea or two."

The day looked like it might tend toward rain before it was finished. Low flat clouds scudded overhead on their way somewhere, blown from the northwest by a steady wind that had lost its sharp edge and turned damp. The river looked cold and a darker gray when they crossed it. He remembered the first time he'd seen this ford, after three days from the Brazos, stopping to rest the mare, rest himself a few minutes—Ben Turner and Sarah in the wagon, her quick wave, the beginning of his new life.

He felt contentment settle itself in his bosom like a small animal asleep in its burrow.

Ames Bradberry sat bareheaded at his desk, bent over a stack of papers, Gus Meyer adding a log to the potbelly stove in the corner, smoke leaking from it because of the interrupted draft, the odor of the smoke benign and pleasant in the confined air of the room. Bradberry stood up when Hub and Estrella came inside and the sheriff and deputy paid close attention to the woman. Hub figured men behaved just that way everywhere she went.

"Sheriff, this here's Mrs. Duncan, from out west of here." The information caused a reaction in Bradberry, a momentary flaring of his eyes that he just as quickly covered up.

"Pleasure, ma'am. Have a seat. What can I do for you?" He glanced at Hub and sat back down.

Estrella spoke up. "I have only just learned about the man Isidro Mendoza who was brought here wounded. I want to see him."

Hub said, "Is he still over at the doctor's?"

"Yes, he is. We'll walk down there in a minute. Mrs. Duncan, can you shed some light on the matter? He claims no knowledge of who it was shot him, but I'm not sure he's telling the truth."

She broke off eye contact and said, "I'm sorry, but I have no idea."

Hub figured Estrella did have an idea, just like he did, but he kept it to himself.

She continued. "Isidro went with my husband and some others to capture a horse, and when it was done he went away alone. That's what I was told."

"By who? Who told you that? Your husband?"

"Yes."

"That's pretty much what your man said to me. One thing, though—I offered to send word and let you know he was here, and he didn't want me to do it. I know fear when I see it, and he was afraid of that. Any idea why?"

She shook her head. Bradberry watched her for half a minute and reached for his hat.

"Let's go down and see him. Gus, I'll be back in a little while."

A light sprinkle had begun, caught in the wind that had brought it, and they walked the distance in silence, heads bowed against the cold snip of rain in their faces. Hub thought about the horses, and the sheriff read his mind.

"We'll get her introduced to the doctor, Hub, and me and you can come back and move your transportation out of this rain."

They had to wait—Kountz was with a patient, but he came to the front in a few minutes to see the man out, and listened to their story.

"I'll let you in to visit for a little while, Mrs. Duncan. Remember, though, you can't stay long. And I can't offer you much hope that he's going to live through it."

She entered the room behind the doctor. There was no stove in here, and the room seemed cold, but Isidro was well covered with quilts, and the face above the cover was still the man she knew, though thinner and of a color like the river she had crossed coming in. There was an odor in the room like that of an unwashed body, and of the chamber pot beneath the bed.. The doctor touched Isidro's face, patted the cheek, and the eyes opened.

"You have company," the doctor said, then to Estrella, "I'll leave you alone."

She waited for the door to close. His eyes seemed to be trying to focus on her face. "It's me, Isidro."

"Yes?" How thin the voice. "At last a pretty angel."

"I'm very sorry you're hurt."

"Estrella...." His lips were cracked and dry-looking, his tongue too large for his mouth. He worked his lips over his teeth, found her face again, his eyes intent now and pointing like fingers, "Is Robert here?"

"No, I'm alone."

A bit of relaxation in him then, the old smile. "Then...run away together."

"I think you will not run anywhere for a while, Isidro."

"How'd you find me?"

"It's such a long story, we don't have time for it, but no one else knows. Robert doesn't know you're here."

"And you won't tell him?"

" No. Is he the one?"

"I didn't see who shot. Coming back for one more kiss. Never made it."

"You have to forget about the kiss. For a moment I lost myself, lost my place. It seemed that the old life had returned to me, but that's not possible. I am a married woman, and that's how I'll remain."

"Rich man's woman."

"And there is the old bitterness, and we can't have it like that with you sick and dy..." She stopped.

"Not dying. Forget about that."

"So you will live, then. And come looking for revenge on Robert?"

"I told you, I don't know who did it."

"And I don't believe you."

She told him about the happenings around the stallion, though sometimes he seemed to doze away into sleep while she talked, not hearing her words, but she kept on in a monotonous low whisper as if she could save him by keeping his attention. It seemed to her she'd been there only moments when the doctor came again and she had to go away.

After he walked her to the front door Kountz stood watching through his window as she went down the street to Bradberry's office. Rain had begun to fall harder and he didn't envy the ride she'd soon be making back out to Anderson's place and that brother she'd described. Not exactly the kind of ailment he could treat, still it would be interesting to look into behavior of that sort—a branch of lunacy more in keeping with nighttime seances, ghosts and full moons than the science he had followed all his life.

If the rain kept up, the road would be even worse tomorrow and possibly his buggy would be stranded in town. Now that she was out of sight he began to think so. It was very hard to say no to a beautiful woman, even harder to a beautiful, sad woman.

Hub carried a slicker in his saddle roll and was glad to see that Estrella had some protection, too—an India rubber affair that her head fitted through, and which covered all her body like a cape. The rain had been a surprise. But the fall had been dry this year, and in the long run the muddy road meant a better springtime when it came, greener grass and fatter cattle.

What a great difference there was between this woman and Robert Duncan. She was all courtesy and decency, a good deal like Sarah, but without the fire that smoldered in his blonde wife. Estrella seemed, on close examination, to be something lovely and wild that had been tamed by a harsh hand, maybe to remain that way, like she'd thrown away part of herself.

Duncan was one who got his way with things. Hub hadn't run across a man like that since his army days. There had been officers who would send you into a hellfire to die or not to die, and it didn't matter to them either way; men who had removed themselves from the softer cares of the heart, like those who sent his brother Lynn into the sure death of Gettysburg and his grieving parents into their graves on the Brazos.

He didn't think so much about those matters anymore in his new life and new home. He tried to leave it to the past. Anyway, you couldn't think your way through it all, how an honest pioneer family that never owned another man had lost itself in a slaveowner's fight over rights that nobody should ever have. He got a deep breath that felt clean in his chest and brought himself back to this present moment, to the rain and the sound of the horse's feet in the wet clay of the road.

They'd stopped long enough at Harper's store to pick up some of the supplies Sarah had asked for, those that were wrapped or packaged well enough to hold out in the rain. James had been in good spirits.

"You ought to build yourself a Sunday house, Hub, much time as you're spending in town lately." Some ranchers did that—put up a town house for wives and children and the rest of their large families to stay in when they made their trips to church on Sunday. It was a practice that a few men strived for, like riding the best horse, something for other men to envy.

"Reckon not, but I will take some of your coffee beans back home with me, and I believe it will be quite some time before you lay eyes on me again unless it's you does the traveling."

"Can't tell," he said, and there was new light in the man's eyes. "Maybe I'll bring some company for a visit one day."

Hub didn't reply to that remark, but it was plain what James meant. It was good to see his friend happy again, but a little worrisome, too. Would the pretty woman treat him well? No good to worry about it, it was James' life. All Hub could do was wish him well.

Another pair of eyes observed the two riders leave town. Jezzie Clawson had just finished with a customer and walked with the woman to the front door of the shop. She recognized the Anderson man who'd come in the store recently. The other figure was a stranger to her, small enough to be a female, but hard to tell in the rain.

The weather had brought business to a halt this afternoon. The last cumtomer had been the only one inside the store in hours. She sat down behind the counter she'd installed in the back and fidgeted with some sheets of paper there, making marks then going back, unsure, to check again. After an hour she sighed, put it all away, got out of the chair and went to a closet.

From it she took a rubber garment, heavy and smelling a bit of oil. Not fashionable at all. She'd worn it horseback many a wet day, but it would do. It wasn't far to walk. There was little danger of turning away business on a day like this. She reversed the card so that it said closed, set the lock and stepped into the waning day.

Doors were shut and shades pulled against the cold and rain. Her footsteps sounded on the boardwalk for a short distance, then she picked her way through the mud of the street, crossed it and went away southward. At some distance now from the cluster of businesses in the middle of town she began to pass houses set here and there, the homes of merchants, and this was where the churches were built, too, out of sight of the saloon and what went on there. Beyond was the south fork of the Llano river and the quickly-rising country that led away toward San Antonio and Mexico.

A small wood house stood alone in a grove of live oak and mesquite trees. It was built of boards and batts, whitewashed, and even in the rain looked well-tended. Smoke, in grays and whites, rose from the red brick chimney. There was a front entrance to the house, and a walkway that led down the side to another porch and another doorway. She looked around once, saw no one, and followed the path. She felt the cold scratching at her face, smelled the oil of the raincoat, the clean rain and the scent of oak leaves. Under the protection of the porch overhang she knocked at the door. After a minute there were footsteps inside. When it opened, a man stood there, outlined in lamplight. He stepped back without a word, let her come inside and closed the door again.

CHAPTER 29

CHARLIE and Tom got in a half day of cedar chopping and gave up on it after the rain came in. The needles soaked up water and dropped it on you at a touch, and you couldn't stand under one and cut it down without being wet through to the skin.

They gathered their tools and horses and began the ride home.

"Put your slicker on if you want to, Tom. I think I'll leave mine off, already wet like I am. That wind is cold, though. Hope your mama's got a big fire set."

The bull stood in the northwest corner of his pasture, looking bigger and whiter than usual in the dark day. He kept his back to the wind and paid them almost no attention as they rode close to the fence that enclosed him.

Tom said, "Would he hurt you if you was to go in there on foot?"

"I'd rather you stay shy of him, son. He's throwed a hook or two at me since we brought him here. I been thinking about polling him, but I just hate to do it."

"Why do you hate it?"

"Aw, no good reason. I just like the way he looks with them old scary horns. Makes me feel good to see him."

Tom smiled at that and shook his head, but didn't reply.

They brought the horses inside the barn, out of the rain.

Charley said, "You go on in the house, son, get on some dry clothes. I'll take care of Speedy for you and wipe these axes down so they don't rust."

He enjoyed working in the barn. It was almost another world in there, with the smells of hay and corn, and of the leather harness on the wall; the strong look of the steel plow and harrow, and the other tools that hadn't seen use yet but would see plenty come spring. That would be something all right, his own corn field, maybe some sorghum. I know how it feels now, Colonel Buford Boone, to stand on your own land and sleep in your own house and think about the crops you'll plant on the other side of winter. Buford Boone lay in a soldier's grave years after he and Charlie had grown up together, played in the sandy yard together until the day Charlie went into the fields of the Boone plantation to earn his keep.

He heard the side door open, and it was Tom again. "Mama wants you to come in the house."

"Tell her in a minute. There's still some things I need to do."

"She said to hurry up. Somebody's waiting on you."

Rose and the other woman sat in chairs near the fireplace when he came in. Tom had changed out of his wet clothes and stood near his mother with his back to the flames. The day was dark enough that lamps had been lighted and there was a soft, moving radiance on the walls, and the scent of coal oil. Tom had hung his wet hat on a peg by the door and it dripped water into a small puddle forming on the floor. The heat in the room met Charlie like an old friend and made his legs weak with the joy of it.

Rose turned in her seat and said, "This here's Ivy."

In the time it took Charlie to put on dry clothes Rose had

made coffee and it waited for him in her hand fixed just the way he liked it. He stood beside Tom and sipped the coffee, felt the fire through the fabric of his pants and against the skin of his back, the heat moving underneath his shirt-tail like a comforting hand.

The woman had said almost nothing to him, but from Rose's face he knew the news she'd brought couldn't be good. She must have walked there. He recognized a dress of Rose's on her, though it barely fit, her being much larger than his wife. He could smell something cooking from the other room, cornbread and a pot of beans, maybe. He was hungry and his mouth watered at the thought of the meal they'd soon have.

He looked from Rosabelle to Ivy. "What is it?"

Ivy kept on staring into the fire. It was Rose who told him, "She's walked all the way here from the ranch she was working on. Them McGee people."

"That's the ones cut our fence."

"They the ones going to burn us out, Charlie."

He glanced at the boy. "Listen here, Tom, maybe you don't need to be listening to this, because there ain't nothing like that going to happpen." But Tom stayed where he was.

Ivy looked away from the fire. "They hired a man, call him a regulator. What he is, is a gunman. They makin' plans to come on Sunday night. I don't know what all they may do, but Mister William, he intends to run you clear out of the country. And just so you know, he hung people in Mississippi."

How familiar it all was. "Miss Ivy, I spent most of my life afraid of folks like McGee. But times has changed. How come you out here with him? He ain't your master no more. You a free person, just like me and my family. You don't have to be his servant no more."

Her eyes went to the floor. "I raised him. And he was a good child. My sweet boy. But they changed him, made him like theyselves." A long pause. "Didn't seem like there'd be no life for me back there when he left."

"Don't he know you're here?" He couldn't keep the suspicion out of his voice.

"No, sir. He wouldn't of let me leave and tell you. I run away from him, gone for good. I won't see no more of it."

"How'd you know where to find us?"

"All I knew was to come south til I run into that bob wire fence and I done it without taking a thing but the clothes on my back. I can hear the little bit of doubt you got, but I'm telling you the truth, and I have give up everything to do it. I can't ever go back."

That night when Rosabelle climbed into their bed she said to him, "I made her up a nice pallet by the fire. She'll be just fine til morning, but lord knows what she'll do then, poor woman."

"I don't mind if she stays with us a while. She got nowhere else to go."

"All right, Charlie. I got some material, I could sew her a dress or two, so she's got some clothes to wear."

"That'd be good. She made a big sacrifice to save us."

"But you ain't going to leave here, are you?" Her voice had gone flat.

"You know I ain't, Rose."

"What you plan to do about the things she said? We better tell the sheriff. There's three days til Sunday."

"Sounds logical, only it won't solve nothing. They'd leave us alone if Bradberry was here, but they'd just come back some other time, and we wouldn't know when they was coming. You see? This time we do, so we can be ready."

"How do we get ready for something like that?"

"Take you and Tom and that Ivy woman to the Turner place first, and then—"

She hissed at him like a stepped-on rattler. "You ain't taking me nowhere, Charlie Boone! Nowhere! You hear?"

"But you wanted to leave, Rose."

"No, I wanted us to leave. All of us. If you come, too, that's fine, but I ain't leaving you here alone, and Tom won't either."

He put his arms around her and held her that way until her body relaxed, and he said, "All right. What I have to do is ask for help."

CHAPTER 30

HUB had put off work this morning. The ground was wet, though the rain of last night had stopped. There were yearlings that needed his attention, thorns and cuts that needed doctoring, and he had to do something about the dun's carcass, too; either burn it or haul it away from the house. He'd get to it, but he needed an hour or two first with his wife and daughter. Happenings outside this house had been too much lately, left his head in a spin with too many people in and out of their quiet life. As much as he wanted peace, there'd been the argument with Sarah to start the day. But that was over, thanks be, and they'd hugged and made things better for today at least.

The argument had been about Felipe. Looked like he'd be staying with them for a few days until his sister could smooth things over with her husband. She had nowhere else to leave him, and besides, the doctor was coming out from town to see the young man, talk to him, try to understand his lunacy. But it worried Hub, riding off to work and leaving Sarah and Marie alone with a very strange man who claimed to read horse's minds.

Estrella Duncan had left before daylight to make the ride home. They'd kept her pony in the corral the night before, so Hub hadn't had to chase him down. She'd had little to say before going away this morning and hadn't talked much on the ride from town, either. She seemed to have a lot on her mind.

Well, of course she would, with the husband yet to deal with, and the brother. Too hard a life for any woman.

Sarah had just taken Marie into the other room to change her when a call came from the back yard. "Hub! It's Charlie Boone!"

While Charlie explained what had brought him Sarah cleaned the kitchen, glancing at the two men now and then, but holding off comment.

Hub said, "I reckon we'd better go over to Ben's and let him know. With John and Falling Rock there's six guns among us and I believe that's plenty of defense."

Her voice shook a little, whether from fear or anger Hub didn't know. "I don't see why you can't just leave for a while, Charlie, let the mess blow over."

"It won't blow over. They'll take my land. I won't never get back on it."

"You should let the law handle it."

He sighed, got to his feet. "I don't want to cause no trouble for you. I better go back home."

Hub stopped him. "No, it was the right thing, coming here. Me and Ben told you we'd help you through this and you can be sure we will."

She said, "Anyway, I wish you'd leave my son out of the fight."

Hub put his arms around her, tried to offer comfort. "I don't know what's changed in you, but you are asking too much. I'm trying my best to stay whole for your sake, for the baby, but I can't turn away from a friend in trouble. What would that make me? As for John, he's your son, but he's not a child. He's a grown man and the son of a Comanche fighter. You think he'll hide from trouble?"

She laid her face into his shoulder. "Ames Bradberry is a good man. He'll stop it."

"Ames is just fine. He's done his best. But he can't do more unless the law gets broken, and when it does it'll be too late. You see? It's up to us."

Minutes later she watched them ride off, angry at herself because she felt so afraid. There was always danger in this life of theirs, and to keep on demanding that her men back away from it was the wrong thing. She knew that, and she knew this very willingness of Hub's to fight was the first thing she'd noticed about him, the first thing she'd loved. In that way he reminded her of Two Hawks.

It was this second chance that made her afraid, this second life, second love, when she had expected to live out her days alone with only memories. Hub, Marie, all of it so precious she felt that the loss of even a piece of their life together might destroy her. Her hands were clenched into fists. She held them up before her eyes and willed them open, stretched her fingers, flexed them, and in the silent room where the only sound was the snap of burning wood in the stove, said, "All right, Hub. All right."

* * *

Estrella met two riders when she was halfway home, Elmo and another of their hands. Even from a distance she could see the relief on Elmo's face.

"Mr. Duncan sent us this way, couple of others to the San Saba. I sure am glad to see you, ma'am. Scared us all, you gone."

"Well, as you can see, I'm fine and have no need for care-takers." She offered them no explanation, didn't even slow her pony, rode through them and let them catch up. They posted themselves on either side, the three horses abreast, the road just wide enough to accomodate them, as though to protect her or maybe prevent her from going into the trees.

Elmo said, "What about that brother of yours? He's gone from home, too."

She shrugged. "I don't know. That's where I've been, looking for him."

"It appears like he turned the mustang loose."

"Did he? I wouldn't know."

"He ain't with the horse, because we tracked that mustang a long ways before we lost him, and we never seen no sign but hoofprints. You don't think he would have rode him, do you?"

She traveled on without comment, as though she hadn't heard.

Her husband had spent the day, as he'd spent the day before, emptying and filling a tall glass with whiskey. All his emotions had sputtered out, died like a prairie fire run short of fuel, and all he had now was the sense of blackened fields inside himself where something fine had grown before, a strength, a power that seemed lacking in other men. The whiskey didn't help, and he wouldn't have cared if the bottle ran dry, but it was habit now to lift the glass and sip at the amber liquid, feel its hot slide down his throat. That act seemed the only reality left in his life.

And all because he had, out of generosity, permitted his wife to house her insane brother here. Because he had trusted and loved a woman now run away like the no good mustang, without warning, without so much as a written note of explanation. And his beautiful black hunter dead, the life bled out of him fighting the runty cur of a stallion.

Noise from the back of the house caught his attention and through the window he saw Elmo leading Estrella's pony toward the ranch outbuildings. Did that mean he'd found her? Where was she, then? He tried to stand up and only lodged himself deeper into the stuffed chair. The back door opened and closed. Footsteps approached and there she stood, her hair mussed, her clothing dirtied, face dusty from a long ride somewhere, but still beautiful. He felt the same reaction to that beauty as always. Not trusting himself to speak, he waited.

"Yes," she said, "Felipe set the animal free. He told me so and then he ran away."

"Where you been?" Not terribly slurred, but difficult.

"Trying to find him and bring him back."

"Can't come back. Dead, cause of him."

"You should go to bed, Robert, sleep the whiskey off. You can barely talk."

"No note."

"From me? No, I didn't leave one because I didn't know when you'd be back or when I would, but I thought it would be sooner than this."

"Where you sleep? Last night?"

She tried to come up with an answer that would put his questioning to rest. "Junction City. I wanted the sheriff to know about Felipe if anybody sees him."

"Felipe." The name trailed from Robert's mouth like a whispered curse and he laid back his head and closed his eyes. She watched his breathing change, deeper and slower, watched sleep come over him, decided to leave him there. She took the empty glass from his hand and set it on the floor.

CHAPTER 31

DOCTOR Alfred Kountz thought better of his promise to visit the stricken young man, the Duncan woman difficult to put out of his mind. The day after the rain was not a very busy one in his office, and at length he decided to brave the muddy road. It would be something of interest in the midst of much that was not, and Estrella's acquaintance was somethng he would enjoy continuing. He saw to it that the recovering Isidro had the things he needed for an afternoon alone and made an arrangement with Gustave Meyer to look in before dark, just in case.

The road west was not half as bad as he'd feared. The ground was thirsty and had quickly absorbed the rain, left little standing. Sunshine was abundant, the day nicely warmed. At the end of his ride he found Sarah alone with the baby girl, Hub gone off to her father's place. The brother was said to be somewhere nearby, though Sarah didn't offer to help find him..

The doctor managed to achieve nothing but muddy boots walking after the horses, where Sarah had told him he might find the man. He grew tired of searching and was returning to the house without any success when he saw the two riders. One of them was the colored man who was in that scrape over the fence cutting. That one paused his horse for only a moment before continuing, but Hubbard spied the doctor walking in the muddy pasture. He came at a trot and Kountz explained his presence.

"No use you tromping around in the mud. Go on back to the house. I'll ride down a ways and see if I can locate him."

Kountz waited by the woodshed. He enjoyed the feel of the sun on his head and shoulders while he scraped the mud from his boots as best he could, and soon Hub and the mare were in sight again. A figure on foot walked beside them.

"I told him you wanted to talk to him, but I can't guarantee he'll listen." Hub dismounted and led the mare toward the barn. "You're welcome to come in the house where you can sit down."

"It's nice here in the sun. Why don't we talk right here?" He said to Felipe and waited for a response, getting none. There was a rough look about Felipe, long hair, barefoot, the dark burn of sun on his skin.

"Your sister asked me to come see you."

"Estrella? She's not here."

"No, but I came at her wish."

"But what can I say to a man like you? Don't you know I have no sense?"

* * *

Isidro Mendoza had not felt as sleepy since the woman's visit. A sick man still, it had been exciting anyway to be so close to her, listen to her voice. Though she had gone, the feeling of excitement stayed, always there, so that when he dozed into sleep it would whisper in his ear and he would wake again thinking of her. He smiled, and felt the smile turn down with the other thing he thought about, worried about—would she tell Robert he was alive? Where she had found him? Estrella was a better woman than most, but a woman still. Somehow, even not meaning to do it, she would tell her husband, or he would guess it, and what then?

What could he do about it when Robert came for him again? There would be no luck next time. That man would be sure to finish the job. Was it possible to leave here? He tried the strength of his torso and it hurt him down low from the shooting and cutting, but he raised up a little in the bed and then the strength ran out of him all in a rush and left him weak and sweating in the cold room. Maybe not today.

So he couldn't leave, he wasn't well enough to defend himself, and his only choice was one he didn't like.

Down the street Gus Meyer remembered he was supposed to check on the doctor's patient. As he started for the door Bradberry looked up from his writing. "Where you headed, Gus?"

The deputy told him.

"When's the stage due?"

"Oh, I'm not sure. Week or two, I think. They ain't exactly regular these days."

"I don't want to wait that long. Hate to ask you to make a trip, but I need you to ride down to San Antone and send off a telegram."

"Okay by me, Sheriff. I don't mind."

"And I want you to wait there for an answer. A reasonable length of time, anyhow. Overnight if it comes to it."

"Sure."

Gus was a good man, always willing. "I'll have it finished by the time you come back. Leave real early in the morning and you can be there before dark. Your horse fresh?"

"Ain't been saddled in a week."

"Good. Well, then, you go ahead with your chore."

Gus thought about the trip as he walked over to Kountz's office. He was looking forward to the journey. The hills had turned out some color this year in the red oak and the sumac and the weather was just cold enough to keep the horse's energy high. He would enjoy the sights along the way. Mendoza was awake and seemed glad to see him.

Gus said, "Anything I can do for you til the doctor comes back?"

Isidro had made up his mind. "No, I'm okay. But there is something I need to tell you about."

After he heard the story Gus left to inform the sheriff what he'd just learned. There was always more than enough trouble around here, he decided.

"I don't know what this Duncan fellow looks like. Do you?"

"No, Sheriff, I never even heard of him before."

"Well, for now the main thing is, we can't let him come into town and shoot Mendoza where he lays. Maybe the wife won't tell him, but I reckon we ought not to bet on it. Anyhow, I'll worry about it. You go on and get yourself ready for your trip. Here's the message I want you to send."

Gus took the sheet of paper and folded it to fit his shirt pocket. He walked out of the front office to the back where the cells were. He'd locked a drunk in one of them early this morning. The man ought to be sober by now.

Telling the deputy about the shooting had left Isidro feeling tired and unhappy. Now he was cut off from the revenge he wanted, but when he was honest in his thoughts he knew it was unlikely he would ever have done it, anyway. Isidro didn't have the coldness in him that the other one had. Probably he couldn't gun Robert down as he wished to do even if he had the opportunity. Now he had to consider the business of the law—the charges against Duncan; maybe a trial. They would never judge him guilty, a rich man like that, and with no witnesses. It would be a waste of everybody's time.

He slept and when he woke again it was because of the doctor's hand on his forehead.

"No fever," Kountz said. He held a lamp in one hand and in its aura there was someone else.

"Felipe?"

"That's right," the doctor told him. "He agreed to come stay with you when he learned you were here. What do you think about that?"

"Is he still crazy?"

"Maybe a little. Who's to say? Come closer, Felipe. Say hello to your friend."

He came near the bed, but said nothing, observing Mendoza silently.

"Did you bring some tequila?"

Was that a smile? He shook his head. "No tequila."

"Ah, you talk again. Well, then, I'm happy. Anything is possible."

CHAPTER 32

RAIFORD Clawson led the way, erect in the saddle as he always rode, elbows tight against the sides of his body, hips moving in rhythm with the horse, ascending and descending the hills of loose rock where there was no track to follow. But it was south she had headed, so he kept on in that direction until they came to a narrow draw between hills where soil had settled in, and then it was easy again.

William McGee had stayed a few lengths behind all the way and their ride had been a silent one until now.

"I thought she was one I could trust, but there's a lesson for you, Clawson. She's headed just where I told you. They can't be relied on."

Raiford didn't comment, but it seemed to him that the man sounded like a ten year old kid who'd just been disappointed bad.

Sure enough, as they worked their way down a hillside through thick cedars and came out in the clear a few minutes later, he picked out the touch of light reflected off stretches of wire. And he found the spot where she'd crawled between strands and continued on.

"This is as far as we go, unless you want to cut it and ride through."

"Not today. We'll save that for the next visit."

And so they rode home, Mcgee looking to Raiford small

and lost on top of his Kentucky racehorse. Raiford was beginning to doubt that this was a job he wanted, but the money sounded good, and he needed it. He had questions that nobody was going to answer. This Ivy woman running off was one of them. Easy enough to see the boss man was upset, but the woman was not a slave, after all. She could leave if she wanted. Must be that she was carrying information to that black squatter about the raid. That seemed to be what McGee thought. If so, the Sunday night party he'd heard talked about could go either way—the squatters could pack up and leave, or else maybe they'd get some guns together and defend themselves.

Raiford didn't mind a fight, but these people probably didn't have much fight in them. Too used to giving in to the white man.

* * *

The stallion was still there. It looked like Hub had himself another horse, whether he wanted it or not, but the mustang wasn't one he desired to keep. He supposed it was possible to lead the animal back out to the mesa where he'd been captured and turn him loose there, but there was no guarantee he wouldn't just follow Hub back home. He watched the pieced-together remuda—the jenny, Mendoza's horse, his mare and the dun mustang, grazing dry grass in the distance. Easy to see even this far away that the dun favored his injured foreleg. A trip would be hard on him until the leg finished mending. Duncan must have hit him with a stick or something else that bruised the bone.

Duncan. He'd kill the stallion if he found him here. Was Duncan the legal owner? Hub decided against it. There was no brand on the horse and Duncan had stolen him, anyway.

Stolen the freedom that Hub and Charlie had given him. Well, however you put it, the rancher had no right to call the stallion his. Hub could catch him and brand him right now, claim ownership and nobody else could take him. It wasn't anything he wanted to do, but it might save the wild pony's life.

The mule had been companion to the line-back dun, and so it seemed right to have her pull the wooden sled. It was an affair he'd built when he was hauling wagon-loads of lumber for their house. Two wide beams served as runners, their noses sawed at an angle to slide over rocks, and they were connected on top by another dozen heavy boards cut two by six inches, making a surface of about four feet by six. He used it to haul wood or move rocks out of the pasture; whatever heavy loads needed handling.

The dead horse smelled bad and could hardly be recognized as the animal it had been although for some reason the buzzards and varmints had left the head intact except for the eyes. It was a stench you never got used to, but it was common enough on any ranch, where death was a frequent visitor, the constant enemy of a man trying to feed his family and pay his taxes on profits from the land. Hub worked the carcass barehanded; no use ruining a pair of gloves, and he hated the feel of the cold flesh that tore apart as he pulled the bones into place on the sled. The jenny gave him no trouble, standing quiet through two loadings and pulling with vigor the half-mile to the spot he'd decided on—far enough to remove the smell from the house and barn. The birds and coyotes could get to it there and speed up the time when there'd be just bones to mark the place and the scent of bluebonnets in the spring.

He left the sled in back of the barn, where fresh air, rain and sunshine could have their way with the stains that had soaked into the unfinished wood. Hub took a fresh bar of Sarah's lye soap and brought the wash pan from the porch into the back yard where he took off his shirt and scrubbed his hands and arms over and over again, thinking all the while of Robert Duncan, a man who believed it was acceptable to ride onto another man's land and kill his horse. The soap had a keen odor, but it didn't do much to cover the smell of dead flesh, no matter how much he tried.

Sarah made the soap two or three times a year, out of lye that she manufactured by pouring water through wood ashes, and tallow saved from slaughtered stock that she boiled in the lye water over a fire built under their black cast-iron wash kettle.

He went inside bare-chested, chill bumps on his skin, and found a clean shirt. The house was warm, Marie awake on a blanket Sarah had spread on the kitchen table.

"I don't guess she can fall off there, can she?"

"No, I'm watching."

Hub found a chair and let Marie take hold of a finger, felt the strong grip of her hand. He wriggled the finger and made her smile.

Sarah said, "I'm sorry you had to do that job." She was kneading dough for bread, the crock of starter covered by a thin cloth at her feet.

"Yessir, it was a pretty sorry thing." He thought about a cup of coffee, but his stomach was still a little chancy from the smells he'd been working in.

"Is that man going to pay us for the dun?"

"Said he would."

"You don't believe it?"

"Well, I expect he's already forgot about it. But you needn't worry. I have not."

They were quiet for a little while. Hub tickled Marie's pink feet, clean and brand-new, covered by the hem of her long flannel gown. She laughed out loud.

"Now there's something I like," he said. "I sure do like hearing this baby girl laugh."

Sarah smiled at them and set the loaves back to rise. In a few minutes the kitchen would take on the yeasty scent that meant fresh bread for supper. He was glad it was a ways off yet. A man ought to bring a wide open appetite to Sarah's table.

She glanced at him and looked away. "When are Papa and John and Falling Rock coming?"

"Middle of the day tomorrow," he said, searching her face for the disapproval he knew she felt. "We'll need to feed 'em I reckon, before we go on to Charlie's."

"Why so early in the day? Didn't Charlie say they were coming at night?"

"Yeah, but this time of year, we'll only have three or four hours of daylight by the time we get there, and we'll need to set up a watch on the north fence line to intercept the riders, otherwise they'll cut up his fence again, coming through."

"I'm sure you'll know what to do, Hub."

"My thought is, they're expecting an empty house when they arrive, not a line of armed men at the fence. When they see they're outmatched they'll turn back."

William McGee allowed himself a shot of the sipping whiskey that he kept for himself, the second of three bottles he'd brought with him from Mississippi.

What a mess Ivy had left behind her—nobody to cook and take care of the house and nobody to care for the old man. Things he refused to do himself. Instead, he'd drafted three cowhands. None of them was happy about it and they were all liable to quit. After this raid his next effort would be to find and hire some permanent help in the house. A disagreeable task, when once you simply walked among the slave shanties and pointed when you required help. Now one must ask, and then argue wages.

An hour later he inspected those items the men had readied—the rough wooden cross, sharpened on the bottom for driving into the ground, the flask of coal oil for the burning, the torches of wood and dry grass they would use to light the night. The hanging noose he had tied himself.

Raiford had seen plenty of this back in Missouri. He hadn't cared for it then, and felt the same now. An armed fight was one thing, but this— "Only thing missing here is the robes," he said.

"If we had time I'd find those as well, put the fear of God into these people."

"What time of day you want to leave?"

"Soon."

McGee walked back toward the house. Raiford watched him go, thinking he was positive now he didn't like this job. He didn't mind the trip over there and back, or cutting the barbed wire. He'd cut plenty of wire before, never liked the stuff and never would. But this other business—flaming crosses, hanging ropes—no, that was something he'd never liked.

William had a cup of tea that he had to prepare for himself and sat down thinking of his plans for the night. Maybe Ivy had done him a good turn after all, alerting them. They'd be getting ready for a raid tomorrow night. "But I'm coming for you tonight," he said to the empty room.

CHAPTER 33

WHATEVER clouds there were had come together in the center of the sky, opening the western horizon for the sun. While the men rode on their journey the afternoon warmed, but no one removed a jacket because the day stayed cool in the shadows. By the time they reached the fence line, taking care, making sure no guard was on it, the sunset had begun spreading itself like some bird proud of its feathers, across the open sky, over the trees and grasses, over the barbed wire, even, so that when two men dismounted and cut away their passage it looked to Raiford like the whole great universe was putting on a show.

They continued south through the ranch, found cleared spots where acres of cedar had been cut and piled for burning, startled half-wild bunches of cattle, and as the last of the sun's light began to fade they reached the bull's pasture, saw the big animal standing in his corner.

William said, "On the way out tonight, shoot every head of stock you see. But not now. It would just alert them."

Raiford felt a sinking in his stomach. Kill that bull? For what reason? A big, beautiful thing like that. He was willing to face other men and fight them, willing to shoot a cow and butcher it out for supper. But this? Like coyotes killing off sheep for the fun of it.

The little man swung off his horse and said, "We'll wait here until good dark."

They rolled smokes and found resting spots. Raiford sat alone with his back against an oak. McGee walked toward him and knelt in a pile of leaves, an unlit cigar between his teeth.

"I don't really know much about you, Clawson. Sorry we haven't had time to get better acquainted. How do you happen to be here with your gun for hire?"

"Well, sir, I ain't exactly sure you've put it like it is. I didn't come looking to hire out for this sort of thing, it just happened to be what you had."

"Understood. I know you've come from California. You mine gold there?"

"I bought out a claim from some fellers. Made a little money, then lost it."

"Came home broke, eh? Lot of men leave California with that story."

"I guess they do." No reason to tell the man this wasn't home. Raiford had stopped using that word, ever. If he had to pick a place to call home he guessed it would be Missouri, where they'd be happy to hang him for showing up.

McGee got to his feet. "We'll go in pretty soon."

Raiford felt relieved when the little man walked off. He didn't like him, didn't like being civil to him. Poor time for a change of heart.

Charlie liked to clean the axes every night. The axe heads would get that cedar sap built up on them, and then when the two of them stacked piles of the cut trees it would get transferred from his and Tom's hands to the axe handles, and everything got sticky. So usually after supper, when he had plenty of time, he would come out here to the barn and use an old rag and some coal oil and get them ready for work in the morning. The crosscut saw, too. Sometimes Tom helped him, sometimes Rosabelle laid claim to the boy for other purposes. Tonight she had him cleaning up the kitchen while she and Ivy cut out material for the dresses they planned on sewing.

One of the hounds started baying, probably a fox looking for a chicken. He paid it no mind, kept on cleaning the last axe handle, but the noise didn't die down. Another hound joined in and it was becoming something he would have to go see about. He wiped his hands on a clean rag and his heart began to beat faster.

All the guns were in the house.

Ivy had said Sunday night. She had been sure about that. But the McGee fellow must know what she'd come to tell. Charlie understood too late, knew they'd been fools, knew what was about to happen.

He went through the barn door at a run just as rifle shots rang out in the night air and dogs howled as they were hit. Tom had the kitchen door open when he reached it, and once he got inside the boy dropped the bar across it.

"We barred the front door, too," Tom said, and handed Charlie's .30/.30 to him. "The magazine's full." Charlie jacked a shell into the chamber. Through the front windows he could see moving lights, and one light stationary close to the house. Something burning, the smell of coal oil. He edged along a wall and got closer, saw it was a cross, a burning cross standing in his yard, flames off it climbing high as a tree.

No lamps were lit inside the house; the room where he stood was dark. "Rose? Where are you?"

"Back here loadin' the other guns." There was a shotgun

and a pistol in the bedroom, and Tom had a rifle, so they could defend the windows if they had to. He could see the dark shadows of two dogs lying still in the light of the cross. The other one must have run off. He didn't blame the dog. He'd like to take his family and run off, too, if there was anywhere to go.

Fire and flame could be many things, friend or foe—friend like the fire in the hearth that had warmed this room while his wife worked at sewing a dress, or foe like that fiery thing outside, a symbol of goodness with the devil's tongue licking at it.

Shadows began moving across the south wall of the room and Tom said, "The barn's on fire, Daddy." And sure enough, when he ran to the kitchen window he saw tall flames already climbing the barn walls, reaching for the roof of it, shoving its way inside where there was hay and corn, a new plow and clean axes, and a barrel of coal oil to liven things up. No way to stop it, even if they could get out there. He saw a tear fall off his son's face and felt a great movement of fear and turmoil in his gut, and unreasoning hatred that stayed with him as he made his way to the front door. They were making Tom cry, scaring his son in the boy's own home where he ought to be getting ready for bed. The two of them had built that barn with their own hands.

He lifted the bar and threw back the door, and there they sat, back a ways from the light of their cross, leaning down in their saddles all easy and calm, like they'd come on a visit. Their eyes reminded him of wolves circled around a dying calf.

When he stepped out on the little porch he felt movement around him and realized that Tom and Rose and the other woman had come outside with him, and they were armed. He nearly smiled, thinking of Rose and how that double-barreled shotgun would knock her backward if she used it. She had it raised, though, and he didn't doubt she'd pull the triggers.

"Ain't you got no flour sacks? You Klan boys ain't in uniform."

Raiford had his pistol out, laid across his saddle horn. There was a lot of firepower up there on the porch. Some of McGee's riders would get killed before they could gun all these people down. He didn't want to see anybody hurt, on either side. He raised his voice.

"Why don't you put them weapons down? Somebody starts shooting, there's going to be an abundance of blood hereabouts."

Beside him McGee said in a low voice, "Stay close," and spurred his mount nearer the house. He raised the noose he'd been carrying.

"I'll give you a week to get out of here, and after that I'll hang you, every one of you, and that goes for you too, Ivy, since you've turned traitor on me."

Ivy had a strong low-pitched voice that carried well in the night air. "Didn't turn on you, Mister William. I turned on that ugly plantation thinkin' you carry in your head. Worst rot there ever was. You go on now and leave these folks alone."

"You people will never learn to think for yourselves. This visit is a good case in point. It didn't occur to you that I would just change my plans from Sunday to Saturday, that I could think one step ahead of you, show up when you didn't expect it. Nobody has to die. Just get out, that's all. I don't particularly desire to lynch you, but I will. Ivy knows I will. She can tell you stories."

He smiled and fell off his horse, tumbling backward over the thoroughbred's rump.

CHAPTER 34

RAIFORD had seen Ivy lift the .44 and fire it, but she'd moved too quickly to stop her. He wouldn't have shot her anyway, being mostly in agreement with the things she'd said, and besides, he didn't shoot women of any color. The way the gun jumped caused him to think she'd missed McGee. But the horse had reared, throwing the man off backward, then, wheeling to run, it had stepped on his prostrate body. Raiford spurred into the darkness, leaning over low, but there was no more gunfire. The other riders had dropped their torches and disappeared.

McGee lay on the ground and wasn't moving. The edge of the porch obstructed Raiford's view, so he couldn't see Charlie's family, heard only a wail of sorrow and knew it came from the Ivy woman. He heard a door slam and another wail, this time from inside, muffled by the walls of the house.

He yelled out, "Can we have a truce here?"

"You burned my barn and killed my hounds. Ain't no trucin' about that."

"We ought to see if McGee's alive."

Charlie answered him. "Everybody get where I can watch you. Keep your guns pointed somewhere else."

Raiford felt almost disappointed when he found that McGee was still breathing.

The other ranch hands dismounted, their sidearms

holstered, showing none of the tension they'd carried before this business commenced. With McGee down there was no aggression in them. One rider, a young man probably not twenty years old, kicked down the still-burning cross and put out the fire.

Raiford could just see the outline of Charlie standing on the porch. "I wasn't joking about a truce, mister. This feller might expire if we don't see to him."

"Don't bother me none."

"Think about this, then—when the sheriff hears about it, is he goin' to hear that your Miss Ivy shot at her boss, or is he goin' to hear that she killed him? To my ear one sounds a little better than the other."

Behind the house, flames had eaten half the barn, had reached high enough in the sky it looked like they'd scorch the stars.

Charlie said, "Before I quit worrying about my wife and boy, and begin to worry a little bit about McGee I better have some kind of sign that you men ain't got more harm on your mind tonight. Anything else you want to burn? Anybody you want to hang?"

There was a murmur of response from the men. Raiford said, "I believe we're through with that. Wasn't a lot of enthusiasm about it to start with except for the boss, here."

Rosabelle came outside and took Charlie's hand. She said, "Tom, go in your bedroom and strip everything off the bed, put an old quilt on the mattress—we going to lay this man on it, see how bad he's hurt. Light a lamp, maybe two lamps. We'll need the light."

Raiford helped Charlie carry McGee inside and stretch him out on the bed. Ivy came over to where he lay and said, "I'll look at him." Her face was wet. "I brought him into this world and I guess I can face what I've done to him tonight."

When they put him down Raiford said, "I'll wait outside with the others."

"Yeah, I ain't asking none of you barn burners inside. Y'all can stay out where it's cold."

It seemed even colder when he came out, after the warmth of the house. He and the other men led their horses and drifted down to the still burning, smoking remnant of the barn. Somebody said, "What we done is a shame."

From inside the line of trees a cartridge slid into place and a voice came up. "You're right about that." Raiford reached for his pistol. He knew the others had done the same. "Touch it and you're dead." That stopped him. He knew the stranger had the drop on them, had probably seen the fire and rode up on the place without anyone noticing. He'd heard that voice before. Couldn't place who it belonged to.

"Everybody lay your weapons down."

Raiford tried to sense if there was just one man out there, or maybe more, but there were no sounds to read. He did as the voice directed, noted that the men with him did the same. They were disarmed now, nothing to do but wait and see. He heard the heaving movements of a horse, the hollow contact of hoofs in the shadows, and Hub Anderson rode into sight, his face plain in the glow of the dying fire.

He said to Raiford, "I had you figured for a better man than this."

"I figured that myself, right along with you. Anderson, is it?"

"That's right. You saved me from that fightin' bull a few years back."

"I remember it well, and I'm sorry about this circumstance."

"Where's Charlie and Rosabelle?"

"In the house. They're all right, too. Nobody's hurt but the man that brought us here tonight."

"I guess that would be young McGee."

"It would. Maybe the dead young McGee. Miss Ivy shot the man and they're looking him over now."

"I need to go talk to Charlie, and I don't want your guns at my back. Clawson, why don't you gather them irons and hand 'em up to me. Here." He reached behind and opened a saddlebag. "Put 'em in this."

Raiford did as he said.

"I'm goin' to ride around in front of the house now. One of you may have a boot gun or you may have a rifle that you've hid away. I don't know, but listen to me—if you come at me with it I'll kill you. And that includes you." He pointed at Raiford.

Hub rode around the house, noted the bodies of the dogs, the shattered cross in the grass, burned black, the burned-out torches scattered here and there. Not much light, the moon just a cold slice in the sky, but there was light from the windows. He climbed the steps and knocked. Tom answered the door.

The boy looked relieved.

Charlie came out of the back. "You must have seen the fire."

"That's right. I looked out the window and the sky was lit up over here. I came on as quick as I could."

"We was dumb, Hubbard."

"I guess that's right. I'm real sorry about your barn."

Charlie shrugged. "Can't be helped now."

"More bad news. They cut some of your north fence."

"Yeah, I figured. How much?"

"We can fix it. I understand McGee's hurt."

"Ivy touched off my big pistol, knocked him plumb off his pony, but what it did was the slug grazed him along one side, then the horse stepped on him, broke a rib or two. Rose and Miss Ivy back there doctorin' him now. You see them rough boys out there?"

"We had a short conversation."

"Notice any dead stock when you rode in? I didn't hear no shots, so I been hoping."

"Not a one. I expect they saved their bullets so they could surprise you."

Raiford and the other men had little to say to one another, but they did come up with an idea that was agreeable to all of them. When they saw Hub again he was leading his mare, carrying the rifle in his free hand. Charlie Boone was with him. Hub took the pistols out of his saddlebags and handed them back to the men, who had some difficulty in the dark figuring out who belonged to which.

The young cowboy who'd kicked down the burning cross spoke up. "McGee always said you was a squatter on this land. I never seen a squatter put up a brick house before."

"McGee's a liar. This is my land. I own it. How much land you own?"

A couple of the men laughed. One said, "Nary a acre is how much."

Hub said, "You men need to go back home. McGee can't ride tonight; he's hurt too bad. They're goin' to keep him here. Where's his horse?"

"Over yonder grazing," Raiford said. "You want to keep the horse, too?"

"No, I'm a little short on everything just now," Charlie said. "Somebody burned my barn."

Raiford again, "We been discussing that. You know, McGee's building a brand new one on his ranch. Piles of sawmill lumber, plenty of nails, whatever you need. We believe he'd want you to have it."

"Yeah? I'm starting to get that feeling myself. What else you believe?"

"He'd want us to haul it over here for you. We could get you enough material to rebuild in three or four trips."

Hub said, "You think he'd want you to rewire the fence you cut?"

"No doubt he would. But he'd prefer us to wait til morning."

CHAPTER 35

GUS Meyer neared the end of his long trip. The answer had come back last night, though he hadn't gone to check until this morning. The ride had left him tired and the hotel bed was soft. His horse, too, had deserved some time to rest and enjoy the oats they fed at the livery stable and Gus had been in no hurry to saddle up and head back.

Before leaving San Antonio he had found a cantina and treated himself to a feed of fresh-made tortillas filled with beans that had been slow-cooked with beef and peppers cut up in them. He could taste the peppers on his breath all these hours later, remembering the meal and the pretty girl who had served him. She had brought him water from their well to cool his mouth and throat as he ate. Now he was hungry again and wondered what he had to eat at home.

He felt as if he'd drowsed through half the ride back, sun on his face and his belly full. Now the night had turned cold and it would feel good to go inside to a warm bed. Of course, the horse came first and he'd do what was necessary, though taking care of horses wasn't second nature to him as it seemed to be with the cowboys and ranch people he encountered.

He forded the south fork and began the trek into town. There was almost no moon. Junction City was dark except for now and then a lamp in a window. As his horse walked along the street in the silent, still dust, a door opened and a quick stretch of lamplight showed at a side door. He saw the silhouettes of a man and woman in the open doorway. They embraced quickly and the door closed. He stopped the horse in shadow and waited as the woman came down the street in a hurry, walking toward the boarding house.

She was well-bundled, but he recognized her. Jezebel Clawson.

* * *

No way to get word to Ben without a long ride and the mare was tired. Hub went inside and closed the door against the night that was growing colder. With the clear sky overhead there might be a freeze before morning. Sarah was waiting. He'd known she would be, leaving as he had, yelling back over his shoulder about the fire in the west, and her not able to know the cause until now.

"They showed up a day early. Burned his barn. That was the big blaze."

"Was anybody hurt? Are you all right?"

He told her about the two dogs, and about McGee.

She made a pot of coffee while he talked and poured two cups full, steam rising off the cup she handed him, the scent of it already a comfort to them both.

"Ran into somebody you may remember, the man that brought me to your ranch after the bull got me."

"Really? I remember him. What was he doing there?"

Hub shrugged. "Hired out to McGee. Gun work, it looks like."

"He was there to run the Boones off? Burn their place?"

"To tell you the truth, he acted like the whole affair disgusted him. I think he had a change of mind in the middle of things when he saw how it was going. Didn't show any fight when I got there."

"It was hard being here, no way of knowing what was happening to you."

"Yeah, Sarah, I knew it would be and I'm sorry, but I couldn't just sit here while it went on."

"No, and I didn't expect you to, it's just...I wanted to tell you it was hard."

"I'll be careful about that from now on; I mean about leaving you alone to worry. I understand what you've been saying all along about it. But tonight..."

"I guess we need to get word to Papa."

"It'll have to wait til morning. My mare's tuckered out and I am, too."

"You could ride that horse of Mendoza's."

"Maybe I will, when I've had some sleep."

But in the morning, after they had breakfast and he went looking for the animals already grazing head down, vapor rising off their backs in the clean, cold start of the day, his mind played with a new thought, not at first in seriousness. Mendoza's gelding was a good-looking horse, and a ride on him to the Bent-T would be simple enough.

But the stallion.

It would be interesting to try a ride on him. The limp was still there, not as pronounced as it had been at first. If he'd tolerate a saddle, why not gear him up and ride him, taking it slow. Exercise might be good for the leg. The horse acted like he wanted to be here. He made no trouble. One ride, then. Maybe the last ride, too, because if the dun fought him he would back off and let things be.

Hub got a halter off the wall in the barn and a half sack of corn and walked into the pasture past the stained ground where the line-back had fallen. One by one the horses paused in their feeding, raised their heads and watched him come. The mare began to walk toward him and the rest followed.

Once the mustang shoved his nose into the corn Hub got the halter on him and after a few mouthfuls of grain he came along at Hub's heels. The mare watched them go with a kind of indignant look on her face.

Hub said to her, "Don't worry, gal. I still love you."

CHAPTER 36

HUB kept expecting the stallion to throw a fit, but he offered no resistance at all, and it was easy enough to guide him out of the corral and toward the just-risen sun. It took work with the reins to keep his head pointed right, but that was just a lack of experience, not a lack of willingness. In between beatings Duncan must have taught him a little about the bridle, the bit in his mouth and the touch of reins on his neck. His gait was the best thing about the horse for anybody riding him. Once they got underway he settled into a pace that covered ground in a hurry, despite the slight limp.

The three men had already saddled up. Their horses looked ready to leave. Ben's old hound came out from under the porch and bayed at him a couple of times, then went back to his rest. Ben opened the back door.

"Didn't expect to see you here this morning." He wore his pistol belt and an extra belt of cartridges hung around his neck. John came outside behind him, and the Comanche. Falling Rock was dressed for war in his breechclout, but he wore a shirt, too. There was no paint on his face, though Hub had noted that the Indian's horse carried some decoration in the form of colored handprints on his withers and a rawhide noose around his neck. A Comanche would put an arm through that noose and his heel over the horse's rump and hide from an enemy while he rode in close.

He told them what had happened.

"So we ain't needed after all, I guess," Ben said, and he sounded a little disappointed.

"No, sir. I would've come last night, but it was late and I was wore down."

"Well, we need to be sure Walt McGee understands what that boy is up to. Them hands of his say they goin' to rebuild the barn or sit down and watch while Charlie does it hisself?"

"They talked like it last time I saw them. Might change their minds, though. I'll go back over there and help clean it up. The first load of lumber won't be there for a while yet."

John said, "If you don't mind I'll go with you, visit my ma some and help with the cleanup, too."

The Indian walked past them and studied the mustang. John said, "Rock don't want to go, anyhow. He's had a dream and wants to stay around here."

"Some kind of medicine dream?"

"Yeah, he won't talk about it, but it must've been strong. He's kept quiet all morning."

Ben took off his hat and said, "I wouldn't be much use to you. One-armed carpenters don't do good work. Reckon I'll sit on the porch with Rock and wait for his dream to come true. A man my age needs his entertainment."

Hub said, "I'm ready to go if you are, John."

"Just a minute or two. I have to tell Alta bye."

They shuffled through the back door into the house. The two Comanche women, Alta and her mother, busy putting dishes away amid the smells of bread and coffee mixed with the smoke that leaked from the wood stove.

Hub noticed Alta frown when John told her.

"Stay all night?"

"Yes, I believe I will. My baby sister won't hardly know me if I don't see her more than I do, but I'll come home first thing in the morning."

"First time," Alta said. John grinned and hugged her, looked at Hub.

"Be the first time I was away all night since we got marrried."

Hub had learned that's how it was with women, white or red, and probably black or brown. Took things to heart more than men, or more than men showed, anyhow. Here was this boy, wanting to see his mother, wanting to stay with his wife, unable to do both. Either way, feeling a little burn in his belly, a little pull in the direction opposite where he's riding.

Falling Rock spoke to Alta and looked at Hub, waiting for her to translate his words.

"Say your horse see bad one eye. Big shadow." She pointed to her left eye.

Hub nodded. "Somebody hurt him. I'm hoping he gets better." He had no idea how the Comanche knew about that eye, but these people had lived with the horse for generations. Big shadow. That might explain why the stallion had stayed around his ranch; hadn't run off to the mesa.

Traveling back, he was careful to guide the dun away from branches that might hit the left side of his face, though he hadn't done that on the ride over and had not noticed any problem. After a mile or two it was evident the horse could see well enough to get by and Hub let up on the help that wasn't needed.

John had been quiet. Hub said, "Your wife take some of the fun out of your trip?" John was a grown man. Too late to play father to him, but Hub understood from his own experiences that even a well-grown man could feel lost when it came to living out your life. Especially with the things a woman needed from you.

"I reckon she did." John laughed, making light of it.

"If you want to go back, you better do it while you're still close to home. Sarah won't mind. She's not expecting you anyway."

"No."

And so he left it alone and there was no conversation for a while. Hub noticed that the stallion always stayed a length or more in front of John's paint. Kept that smooth pace, but sped it up when the other one came close. Had to be the leader, even now. Couldn't let another animal out front.

"He's got a limp," John said.

"Yes, probably I shouldn't have brought him. His leg's starting to hurt him, I think."

"You ain't branded him yet."

"No. I don't know that I will." He waited for John to ask why, not sure how to answer, but no question came and he was glad. Hub knew that a lot of men, most men probably, wouldn't worry over this horse—ride him or not, turn him loose, shoot him. In his experience men treated a horse like a tool: a gun or shovel or pick-axe, something to be used, cared for to get the best out of it, then disposed of in the easiest way.

There was somethng closer than that between him and his mare, although he'd never tried putting it into words for himself or anybody else. And now this little stallion. What he truly wished was that the mustang hadn't come into his life at all, hadn't brought Robert Duncan into it. A man saddled a horse and all the while the horse was saddling him, too. Now, branded or not, the future of the animal was on his shoulders. The trip was nearly done when Hub felt hesitations as the stallion came down on the sore leg. He got down and walked the rest of the way.

The smell of Sarah's cooking met them before they came in sight of the house. They shut John's paint in the corral, but Hub turned the stallion back out. He looked at the dun's eye while the bridle was still on, but there was nothing to tell him a shadow was inside it.

She was happy to see John, a little disappointed that her father had stayed behind. "I want to send some food over to Rosabelle," she said. "I imagine she can use it to help feed those men when they come."

"That's thoughtful of you, Sarah. No doubt you're right, and I hadn't even thought about it."

John came back in the kitchen carrying Marie.

"Oh, you woke her up." Sarah reached for the baby, but John turned away and kept her in his arms.

"I want to change her, too," he said.

"Do you know how?"

"Almost. But I have to learn."

Sarah's mind was on the food, the table and dishes. What had he said?

"You what? You need to learn? Why...oh, John."

So that was the reason he'd come—wanted to tell his mother the good news. His face couldn't hold his smile. It seemed to flood all over his body.

"That's right. Alta's got a little one growing."

Chapter 37

ONE of the two wagons was almost emptied when Hub and John rode up, the alkaline smell of burned wood and ashes filling up the wind that blew across the site. The sun went in and out of cloud patches, everything warming one minute, turning gray and cold the next. Raiford Clawson and two other McGee men stacked the lumber they'd brought on a pile of boards already head-high. Easy to see this wasn't their first trip.

Hub said, "I thought you'd wait til daylight to start."

Raiford laughed. "Couldn't sleep. Bad conscience, I guess. Old Jim and R.B. saw me puttin' my boots on and volunteered to come along."

"Where's the others?"

Raiford paused, got out a bandanna, wiped sweat off his face. "They had second thoughts and wouldn't help us," he said. "They're afraid little McGee'll fire 'em, and I figure they're right. Can't blame a man wants to keep his job."

"McGee in the house?"

"Far as I know. Nobody's come out here to greet us. I guess we are not as popular as I generally try to be."

They dismounted and led their horses, the mare and paint, toward the house. Hub said, "We'll be back in a few minutes."

Rosabelle let them in. They carried the food to the kitchen and set the packages down on the table there.

"That's a sweet thing your wife done. Thank her for me."

Charlie and the boy were standing in front of the fireplace. The house seemed too close, too hot, something heavy in the air and on the faces of the family.

John shook Charlie's hand, then Tom's, and said, "I'm awful sorry. Came to do what I can to help."

Charlie nodded. "Well, there's plenty needs doing, I just don't want to talk to them men out there right now. They the ones done it and I ain't ready to lay it to rest yet."

Hub said, "How's McGee?"

Rosabelle spoke up from the kitchen, moving food off the table, "He's mean, is how he is. Ivy's in there now gettin' him ready to go home in one of them wagons."

Charlie said, "Yeah, he's on his feet. Hurts from that broke rib, but she wrapped him tight, and I guess the bullet didn't do more'n just burn him a little and knock him off the horse. I cut him a walking stick, and he gets around with it."

Hub said, "He's a lucky man, then. It's a wonder he lived through it."

A door opened and William came into the room, leaning his weight on the stick and on Ivy. He glanced at all of them but offered no greeting or apology as Ivy helped him to the back door and down the steps.

Charlie said, "Ain't that something? Act like he done us a favor laying in Tom's bed."

The four of them left Rose alone in the house and followed Ivy and McGee. She supported his right side while he tried to climb into the empty wagon's seat. John and Hub stepped forward and lifted him into place.

The rest of the lumber was unloaded in just a few minutes with everybody helping. McGee looked around and motioned to Charlie from the wagon seat. His voice was weak. "I didn't give anybody permission to bring this lumber here. For the record, it's my property, not yours."

Charlie heard him out, and for the first time since the night before there was a smile on his face. He just shook his head and took a few steps back. In his weak voice McGee said to Raiford Clawson, "You're fired. I was nearly killed last night and you did nothing to prevent it. Now you've stolen this lumber from me. You can pick up your pay, whatever's coming."

"No, sir, you keep that money." Raiford had his arms full of short stakes and stopped long enough to spit a stream of brown tobacco juice at the wagon wheel. "If I was you I'd wait to fire the rest, though. Somebody's got to drive you back."

Ivy raised her eyes. "Mister William, you'll be needin' me to take care of you and get you well. Let me come with you. I can't stand thinkin' I hurt you so bad. Please...let me come, too."

He stared ahead for a long minute, then nodded his head and without looking down at her said, "Get in the wagon."

"Yes, sir, and I'll take care of you like always." She was climbing as she spoke and sat in the bed of the wagon, her legs stretched out, her back against the side board.

Charlie said, "Miss Ivy, you don't have to leave, I hope you know that. You welcome to stay."

She shook her head as though in great sorrow. "It was a mistake. A terrible mistake."

CHAPTER 38

JAMES Harper decided early in the morning to return the breakfast invitation he'd so recently enjoyed with Jezzie Clawson. The woman had been on his mind lately. It had been a different attraction than the one he'd felt toward Sarah. Had a different texture, caused a different set of feelings in his chest and belly. Being with Sarah had always left him dizzy and off-balance, unsure of himself and dazzled, like he'd looked into a too-bright sun. He understood now that the lack of balance had been caused by their differences in feeling—him full of open love for her, but Sarah always unsure, always hesitant. Always not in love with him.

But Jezzie, now, the thought of her was a mellow thought, like catching the scent of honeysuckle on a spring wind. Like seeing a candle in the window on a dark night. Could it be he'd found someone at long last to share his life?

He had bathed the night before, but this morning he heated water again on the stove at the back of the store and washed himself, dancing a little in the cold of the yet-unwarmed building, ignoring the leg that didn't like to bend. He felt younger today, hummed a tune as he dressed, watched the time on the tall clock by the door until he was sure she'd be in her store and then he made the walk down the Junction City street.

It was too early yet for customers, but sure enough there she was in back at her little desk, a coal-oil lamp burning for light, dressed pretty like she always was and he went in before he could change his mind, heart somewhere it ought not to be—high up in his throat and about to choke him. The bell on the door jingled when it shut behind him.

"Well, James! What a surprise!" Her voice matched the bell, sounded glad he'd come.

"Good morning. I'd like to buy you breakfast if you have the time."

His invitation didn't have the effect he'd expected. "That's very nice of you, but I don't think I can today." The change had been sudden, a movement from light into something less. She got up from the desk and walked over to him. "I'm sorry."

James couldn't believe how deep and cold the plunge he was feeling, a dive into icy water. Like his whole life had been wrapped up in the need to spend time with this woman and was ruined now and without hope. Like he was seventeen years old again, and destroyed. "Okay, then. I just thought..."

"Thank you for asking."

He heard himself say, "Jezzie, I don't want to string this out—I don't want to find out in a week or a month that I'm wrong again. I want to see you, I want to spend time with you, get to know you. I am beginning to care for you, Jezzie. Tell me what to do."

She turned her back on him and walked a few paces away. She crossed her arms on her chest and bowed her head as if praying. "I can't give you any encouragement, James."

And just like that his world went back to where it had always been. "I thought you felt something for me, too. Listen, I'm sorry to come in here like this. It embarrasses me."

She turned. "You are a sweet man, James. It's true that I like you, but I have difficult decisions to make."

"Maybe I can help."

"No, it's up to me."

"All right, then," and it all happened in reverse, the jingle of the door, the walk back to his store, this time noticing his stiff leg, feeling older, feeling sure now that he'd live out his life alone.

CHAPTER 39

FAR to the west Robert Duncan lay in bed. The effort to sit up was too much for him. Just the thought of putting his feet on the floor, of standing, of walking away from the bed, was too terrible to contemplate. Estrella had slept on her side of the bed after the midnight struggle to move him from the chair. He could see the indentation her head had made in the pillow; but she was gone now, probably in the kitchen making breakfast. The thought of food caused him to feel sicker.

How he'd gotten into bed he couldn't remember. He'd been sitting in his chair drinking, and she had come home, that much he could visualize, some of her conversation he could remember, but then nothing. Now there was the price to pay for the whiskey—dull pain behind his eyes, the feeling of loose rocks rolling in his head when he moved, the tremble of the hand he raised to his hot face. The ugly taste of his tongue. Where was the bottle? Surely not close enough to reach, probably not even in the room. She would have made sure of that. Ah, well, he was not a child after all, to be treated in that manner. A man, yes, a man whose stallion had been killed—killed—by another one wilder, more desperate. But wait, now. The black had been in a fenced pasture. The mustang could have easily run away, yet he had not been desperate to escape. No, he'd paused in flight and gone back to challenge the black, kicked down enough fence wall to get through it, then put his mangy life on the line in what must have been a loud and fierce fight.

A fight no one heard in time, except probably his insane brother-in-law, but even had they heard, it wouldn't have been possible to stop the fight except by killing the mustang, which Robert would have gladly done. Gladly.

He heard Estrella's voice, but she wasn't in the kitchen, she was somewhere outside near the front door. In a few minutes there were steps in the hall and the bedroom door swung open.

"How do you feel?"

"Awful."

She stood there for a moment without saying anything else, looking at him across the room. "The whiskey, I'm sure."

He said nothing at all.

"But not only the whiskey, Robert. The loss of your pretty black hunter."

"I don't need..."

"You misunderstand me, Robert." She came closer to the bed and he saw that she carried a tray. She sat down on the edge of the bed near him, holding the tray in her lap. He smelled coffee. It gave him a fleeting sense of sickness, but then just behind that feeling was desire to taste the hot brew, feel it slide down his hurting throat, feel her hand again on his brow.

"You may have a little fever. All this has made you sick, but I'll help you now if you'll let me." She put the tray aside on the small table beside the bed. With her arms around him she tugged at his shoulders until he allowed her to raise him up off the mattress, and then he swung his legs over the side and sat up. She put the cup in his hand. He swallowed some of the coffee, afraid it would burn his mouth, but she had cooled it for him so that it carried just enough heat, but not too much. The taste of it, the warm feel of it in his stomach, seemed to make the morning better than it had been. He began to feel hungry.

"In a little while, when you finish the cup, put on your clothes and come in the kitchen. Can you eat something?"

"Yes, I think so. I didn't before, but now I think so."

"Good. You needn't hurry."

And he had taken a long time over the coffee and at shaving the dark stubble off his face and neck and in dressing in clean clothing. His eyes were red, but if he stayed away from the whiskey they would clear up. She passed the plate of biscuits that he called scones and he took two of them and buttered them, spread them with the jam she'd made from wild grapes last spring, grapes that hung on vines wrapped around the trees along a narrow creekbed that was a nice walking distance from the house.

He bit into one and made a sound that might have been joy.

"Is it good?"

"My, yes. Suddenly I'm starved. I don't know when I ate last." She had to cook more eggs. He ate with fixed attention, and when he had enough to eat he gave her one of those looks she hadn't seen in a long time—the look of a very young boy on his face, full of something he wanted to give or get, she had never been sure which. But she liked the look, liked remembering it after it went swiftly away, as it did now.

"Thank you, Estrella. I believe you have saved my life." He looked much better, color in his face again, the bent posture of defeat gone.

"Then you owe me, don't you? If I saved your life?"

"Felipe? Don't worry, I won't..."

"No, I'm not thinking of Felipe, or anyone else. I am

thinking of you." This was a talent she hadn't realized she had, twining lies and truths around each other, making it all sound like truth.

"All right then. I owe you."

"Good. Then this is how you can repay the debt. I know a hacienda in Mexico, only a little way from Del Rio on the border..."

"Hacienda?"

"Listen to me, please." She waited a moment and went on, "where they have raised wonderful horses for two centuries, horses desired all over the country. My own father once had not one, but two of them, palominos, a stallion and a mare. He took me with him on the trip he made to buy them, and you have never seen such animals, Robert."

"I have no interest in palominos."

"There were all kinds, blacks blacker than night, whites whiter than clouds, grays, sorrels, chestnuts, every color, every kind you can think of."

"All right. What about it, then?"

"I want us to go there and find another stallion for you."

He took the last swallow of coffee from his cup, watching her over the rim of it. "I had rather thought you'd be leaving me today."

And she had come close to it, thought about it lying sleepless most of the night after she'd moved him from the chair into their bed, listening to his snore, smelling the mist of whiskey from his breath, but in the end she had changed her mind. For the moment. She nodded her head. "I considered it."

He reached for her hand. "Please don't. I can't bear it if you leave."

"If you were always the man you are this minute then

thoughts like that would never come. Don't you understand? Besides, you are my husband. I won't leave." She patted his hand and stood up. "Come outside for a minute."

He followed her out the door and saw the two-horse carriage waiting there, the matched team already in harness, bending after whatever grass they could find. It was packed for a trip. He said, feeling himself smile, "You must have been pretty certain I would agree to go."

"Certain? No, but I hoped so. I want to go away for a little while, leave our troubles long enough to learn to breathe again, long enough for you to feel better, for the hatred in you to burn away. That's not so much to want, is it?"

It had been a long time since he'd felt tenderness toward her. What he felt now was a bit like that, and fear, too. As if he'd been wiped clean of self-assurance, had everthing that told who he was taken away, like a stone pyramid erected inch by slow inch to completion, then struck down in a single blow into nothing more than rubble.

"Why not, Estrella? A trip might be good for us." Immediately as he agreed he felt sorry that he had, but he'd said it and so they would go. No horse would ever replace the black, but perhaps there'd be one that could soothe the pain of loss. And there was Del Rio, and Acuña across the border. It could be interesting to see the towns. Even heathenish border towns would be a nice change.

She allowed herself to relax. This had been easier than she'd expected and maybe he'd been truthful about Felipe and would seek no revenge. The trip would take days, down there and back, and that would be time enough to decide what must be done with her brother.

The young cowboy, Elmo, rode with them for a few miles

down the road heading west toward Fort McKavett, and left them when they turned south on the more lightly traveled track that would take them through the tall hills and softer valleys into south Texas mesquite and prickly pear country. The two horses were full of energy, chewing at their bits.

He popped the short whip in the air, in good spirits like the team.

CHAPTER 40

SHERIFF Ames Bradberry would have felt a little easier if he'd known Robert Duncan was traveling to Mexico. It wasn't something that worried him a lot, more like the buzz of a mosquito in the dark, one you couldn't locate, knowing full well that the bite could come any time. Or maybe not at all. He hadn't really thought about Duncan this morning, though. He had been too busy with other matters.

"What is that? Lye?" He said to the doctor.

"Probably feels like it, but no, just a disinfectant. I'll put a bandage over the cut now and turn you loose."

Bradberry sat on a stool in Kountz's office with his shirt off, feeling like a skinned rabbit, dark-tanned face and hands in contrast with the white flesh of his arms and torso, all reflected back at him from the tall mirror bolted to the wall, the slice across his ribs just a thin line now, something that would heal pretty good. He'd come in minutes ago with blood soaking into his shirt, not sure at all how bad the drunk fool had gotten him.

"What did he use on you, Ames?"

"Oh, it's one of them blamed bayonets the soldiers put on their rifles. You've seen 'em."

"Bayonets? Yeah, more than I've cared to see."

"He had it stuck down in a boot, with his pants leg pulled over it. I never expected anything. He was falling down drunk when they come got me."

"Awful early in the day for that."

"For some of these old boys it's still last night. I hate that dang mirror in front of me, Doc. Turn me around a little so I don't have to look at myself."

"Be a foolish waste of time—I'm nearly through." He wound gauze around Bradberry's chest, overlapping the cloth, then taped it in place and stood back. "I'd like for you to go easy on yourself for a couple of days and give this cut a chance to grow together. It's not deep, and ought not to be much trouble, except you'll be stiff on that side for a while."

Bradberry hated putting the bloody shirt back on, but it was all he had in town and he didn't want to ride home for another one. He buttoned it partially and left the tail hanging outside his pants.

On the way back to his office he changed his mind in mid-stride and walked toward Harper's store. The effort of walking caused the knife wound to sting. He could still smell the chemical Kountz had poured on it. It smelled a bit like whiskey, a not-unpleasant odor, though Bradberry himself was a teetotaler. Not from any moral standpoint, but because he'd never liked the taste of it.

"Howdy, Sheriff, what...?" Harper saw the blood on the shirt, the tear along the left side. "Are you all right?"

"Yeah, I'm fine. Just left Kountz's office. I don't want to ride home after another shirt and thought I'd just buy me a new one if you carry my size."

"I'm sure I do. That happen just now? This morning? I guess it did."

"Yessir. Mean drunk at the saloon, got me with a army bayonet, if you can believe it."

"What happened to the drunk?"

"I should've pistol-whipped him and throwed him in a gully somewhere, but I didn't. No, he was too pitiful. I just stuck him in jail."

"I expect he's a wiser man for it."

"Don't know about wise, but time he pays off his fine and the damage at the saloon he'll be a poor man, I can tell you that."

They found three shirts in the right size and the sheriff decided on a white cotton work shirt with long tails. He put it on standing at the counter and said, "Anywhere you can throw this bloody one?"

"Sure." He took it by a clean corner and carried it to a wooden barrel behind the counter.

"Things all right with you, James? You look a trifle wounded yourself, like my side feels." He pinned his star on the new shirt.

"Sure, I'm just fine." He was trying, but he didn't sound fine. "Make certain you take care of yourself and let that cut heal."

Bradberry was counting out the price of the shirt when the door opened behind him.

James said, "Good morning to you. Something I can help you with?"

The sheriff turned to see a stranger who appeared to be an Indian wearing the clothing of a white man, trail clothes dusty from travel. Under the black hat his face was handsome and sharp, with eyes that took in everything. Two long pigtails hung down his back.

The stranger took off his hat and his skin was a light copper, his eyes lighter than the eyes of an Indian. "Yes sir," he said, "I hope to get some tobacco and some information from you." The words carried an accent, but his English was fluid and well-spoken.

"Smoking tobacco?"

"For my pipe, yes."

"Easy enough." James brought out his tobacco. "What sort of information?"

The stranger glanced at Bradberry and back at James. He was slow to explain.

"There's a family hereabouts that I'd like to find. I have news for them."

The sheriff spoke up. "What's their name?"

He didn't respond to the question. "This family is a husband and wife and two girls, one young, one older. I think they live on a ranch close to this town."

James was nodding his head. "On the Turner place?"

The stranger glanced at Bradberry again, a little uneasy. "I don't know for sure. Maybe I'll come back by later." He reached out for the tobacco, money in his hand.

Bradberry laughed. "No, settle down, now. I know you're wishin' the danged sheriff hadn't been standing here when you walked in, but you can rest easy. You're talkin' about Falling Rock and his folks out at Ben Turner's ranch. And yeah, they're Comanche Indians and they ain't on the reservation, but I don't care. Ben took 'em in and they work for him. They're fine people."

The copper face smiled. "Thank you, Sheriff. I was worried for them. I know their story, you see, how they came to be here, and I wouldn't want to cause trouble. How do I find the Turner ranch?"

James made a quick decision. A ride with this man would beat standing behind his store counter all morning. He would leave a sign and folks could help themselves. "How about I come along to show you the way?"

"Now, that would be just the thing, if you don't mind." He put his hat back on and smoothed the brim.

The sheriff put out his hand. "Let me introduce myself—I'm Ames Bradberry."

"Pleased to meet you. My name's Quanah Parker."

CHAPTER 41

THE hound barked twice with no enthusiasm and went back under the house. Nobody came to the door. James swung down from his Apaloosa and said, "I'm sure somebody's home. Go on and get down."

Parker rode a dark little pony, neither black nor brown but something in between and the Indian didn't fit the animal well, James thought. The man himself didn't look like he fitted the reputation of the last war chief of the Comanche nation, the man who'd held out longer than any other against the U.S. Army. Soft of speech, quick to laugh, there was nothing outwardly fearsome about him, and yet James knew better. They'd conversed on the journey from town, of course, but it was unimportant conversation, small talk about the season, the weather, the abundance of white-tail deer. Whatever the reason Quanah had come, it was still to be told.

While they tied up, Ben came through the door and let it slam behind him. "I didn't see you men ride in. Howdy, James." He put a hand out to the stranger. "I'm Ben Turner."

"Morning, Mr. Turner." And he told Ben his name.

James laughed and said, "Your jaw dropped just like Bradberry's when he heard it."

Ben pulled his face together and said, "Well, I reckon so. That's a surprise to hear. I thought Quanah...thought you...was on the reservation."

Parker took off his hat. He smoothed his hand over his face and hair. "Yes, I am. They gave me permission to make a trip and I'll be going back before long."

"Well, say, I feel very honored you come by. Why don't we go in the house and sit down? Dinner'll be ready sometime pretty soon and I'd be pleased to have you at our table. You too, James, of course."

Alta and her mother watched the men enter. There was a quick recognition of the stranger on Turna's face, which she hid, dropping her eyes, while Alta stared like a child at him.

James said to her, "This here's Quanah Parker, Alta. He's got a message for your family."

The young woman said something in their language to her mother, who nodded, but did not look up. Ben understood that this was an awkward situation. Such a shining guest at an Indian village would be met with much formality, the right words said. He knew for certain, though, that whatever the news, it wouldn't be given to the women, but to Falling Rock, man to man.

He said, "Let's send Rabbit to get her daddy. He's tending to his horse." Alta called her younger sister into the room.

"No," Quanah said, "Let me go find him. I'll talk to him there. She can show me where he is."

The others sat at the table. Alta and Turna brought food but both Ben and James ignored it. Ben said, "Rock's been waitin' on something for days. He had a dream."

James glanced at the solemn women. "Appears to be bad news."

Taking a bandanna from his hip pocket Ben used it to wipe his eyes then put it back in the pocket, stretching a leg out straight and lifting his hip to do it. "I expect it's about the boy."

They let minutes go by in silence and Ben said, "Alta, you may as well put the grub back on the stove to keep warm. I think this will take some time."

When the women finished, Turna said something to her daughter and Alta told Ben, "We want to see my father."

"Well, sure, honey. You two go on. I left him in the horse pasture, reckon that's where the powwow is takin' place."

When they were alone James said, "Maybe I ought to head back to town."

"Ain't you curious about all this business?" Ben got up and brought two plates, set one in front of James.

"Course I am. Just don't want to appear too nosy."

"Let's us dish ourselves a bite to eat. Them women won't be back inside for a while." He spooned his plate full and James followed suit. They were half finished when Quanah came back.

He took off his hat and put it down on an empty chair. "The others are grieving together. I had some hard things to tell them."

Ben got up. "We figured. Well, here, let me get you a plate and you can just help yourself off the stove like we did if that's all right."

"Thanks. I'm very hungry."

He sat at the table and ate in silence, neither Ben nor James willing to ask a question of him. Instead, James asked the older man, "Where is John today?"

Ben told him.

"So the little plantation fool got what was coming to him."

Quanah swallowed the last of his food and said, "John is your grandson? Son of Two Hawks?"

"That's right. Did you know his daddy?"

"Very well, yes, I did. And I remember his wife, the pretty white girl. John's mother."

"My daughter."

"She lives here, too?"

Ben told him the story, noting that James was not comfortable with the telling and not caring much, because it was an old story and high time James got used to how life was.

"And you were the man who killed Two Hawks?"

"Yes, I am that man. He took my arm and I took his life."

"I know you're a brave fighter, then, because no one else could have taken the life of that one."

"I don't know about all that, but I know this—I didn't value my own life at the time and was careless with it. None of us expected such a fight. Nobody could've guessed why he battled us like that, right down to the last breath."

Ben's voice had diminished to a whisper that became silence between the three men at the table. Quanah waited until the silence had been respected long enough and then he said, "And what was his reason?"

Ben shook his head but said nothing, looked away and then back into Quanah's eyes, his own eyes red now, a glimmer of tears in them. "Like any man would, he tried to save his wife and baby boy. And I killed him for it."

CHAPTER 42

JAMES wished he'd gone back earlier. It was hard to watch the emotion on Ben's face. The old man kept that pain hidden away in himself, but now there it was for anyone to see and it caused James to shy away from it, from the knowing of it. There was too much pain here today, in this room and outside, too. It matched the sadness he had carried in his own heart all day. He wished to be somewhere else, not because he felt no compassion, but rather felt too much, felt suffocated by it.

Quanah said, "I bought some fresh tobacco today from Mr. Harper. I'd be happy to share it with you."

Ben said, "I'll take you up on that. My old pipe is somewhere around the house."

"How about you, Mr. Harper?"

"I wish you'd call me James. And no thanks, I don't smoke it." He reached in a pocket and brought out a dark plug and bit off a piece of it. He talked around the wad in his mouth. "But I do love a chew now and then."

When they'd found chairs on the porch and settled in, with the pipes lit and the smoke fragrant in the late fall air, the Indian said, "Would you like to hear the news I brought?"

Ben said, "Well, I imagine it was about their boy. They used to talk about him, and then they quit mentioning his name a while back. I know he'd been on Rock's mind a lot lately and it wouldn't have surprised me if he'd just took off to go and look for him."

Quanah shook his head. "Chaser died at the battle of Adobe Walls. You've heard of it?"

James said, "Sure, everybody's heard of it. Up on the Canadian River in the panhandle."

"That's right. Just a few whites, but well dug in and protected. We went against them with many, many warriors—Comanche, Kiowa, Cheyenne. I led the Comanches and Chaser was with us. Some of the whites were buffalo hunters with their big guns. Do you know how strong the big guns are? One of them shot our medicine man, Minimic, off his horse from a mile away. How can you make war against guns like that? The boy was very brave. He was two days in pain before he died. On the second day he asked me to send word to his father that he had died well. I promised him I would."

Ben said, "If he'd have come here with his folks we'd have made him a place. He could've lived here in peace the rest of his life. Too bad he had to die like that."

"No, you're wrong. He died the way he wished, and with a smile on his face. The way every warrior wants to die, doing battle against the enemy. It's how I should have died. But I'm called on for something else. My people have to learn to live in peace and somebody has to lead them that way. And that's what I do now." He ceased talking and leaned back in the chair, pulling great clouds out of the pipe.

James said, "It must have been hard on Rock, staying here safe with the boy out there still fighting."

"My grandson tells me it's the womenfolk have kept him close. He's a fightin' man, but he also loves his wife and daughters and couldn't make hisself go away from them."

To Quanah, James said, "Is it hard for you to leave the reservation like this? I would have thought they'd keep you there all the time."

The Indian laughed. "Oh, well, I'm a tame Comanche now. I learned English, I keep the people peaceful so they don't make so much trouble. I'll tell you, they like me pretty good at the reservation. Even so, it's hard to get permission to leave. I came this time to visit my mother's grave and the grave of my little sister, Prairie Flower. Do you know the story of what happened to us?"

They nodded. James spit tobacco juice into the yard.

Quanah went on, "I'm trying to get them moved to Fort Sill. My mother, you know, was born white, but she lived as a Comanche most of her life and she never wanted to go back to the white world. The Indians were her people. They say Prairie Flower died from a fever and I think that then my mother decided to die, too. She had no heart to live without us."

Ben said, "It's a wonder my Sarah and her baby didn't do the same."

"Yes, you're lucky. All of you are."

"What will happen now, do you think?" Ben wanted to know. "Will Fallin' Rock settle down here or take off and try something wild?"

"I think what he'll do is go with me to the place we buried his son. It's a long ride there and back, but he'll want to bring Chaser's bones here to be near his family. Will you allow him to do it?"

Ben shrugged. "I reckon so, don't see why not. Won't he need help?"

"No, a father should do that alone. I'll show him the place

and then go on to Fort Sill. He'll bring Chaser's bones home on a travois."

"I've got a little place fenced off with split-rail, just one grave in it," Ben said. "I buried my wife there way back after the raid when they stole Sarah. We can put the boy there."

Quanah said, "My people did that to you. Too much dying, Mr. Turner. I'm sorry for the things that happened to you, and to me. What you've done for this family causes me to feel hope for the rest of us."

CHAPTER 43

HUB was tired. He had let the mare have her head most of the way home. John Turner looked to be holding up a little better. That would be on account of his youth, Hub reckoned, and remembered years when he would've had more energy after a day like this one. Their hands, faces and clothes were black from the charcoal of the burned barn. It had taken a big hunk of the day just cleaning up the mess, and then there was the cut fence to mend, and the loose cows, although John and Tom had done most of that work.

Hard to figure a man like Raiford Clawson, come on a raid with the McGee bunch, changing his mind, hired on now with Charlie to put up a new barn. If you could call Raiford's offer hiring on—he wouldn't take wages, just food and a dry place to sleep. Paying penance for his sins.

John noticed the horses first. "That's Falling Rock's pony tied up at the house. I never seen the other one before."

They unsaddled and turned both their animals into the corral and put out corn. Hub said, "I'll come back out after supper and curry this gal and turn her loose. Yours could use it, too."

"You're right, but I'll wait til I get back home in the morning." He looked at his hands in the fading light. "I hate to go inside before I clean up."

"We'll need some hot water. Likely your mama's got some

on the stove already. Let's go on in and see what's happening with our Comanche friend."

Sarah's face sprang to life when she saw them, then just as quickly turned to a frown. "How did you two get so dirty?"

Neither of them answered the question. Falling Rock sat in a chair dressed in his work clothes, white man's pants and shirt with boots on his feet. Next to him was another man, dressed the same, and also Indian by his looks. Long braids hung down his back. Both men stood.

Sarah stepped in and said, "Hub, John, this is Quanah Parker."

The surprise of the name was almost like a physical shove. Hub felt himself step back from it. Quanah put out his hand and smiled.

"Rest easy, Mr. Anderson. I left the warpath long ago."

Hub said, "Well, you'll admit, though, that a man coming home to find you there is entitled to a second or two of hesitation."

The Indian's voice softened. "Yes, I admit it. And this is Two Hawk's boy?"

"I am, sir. Pleased to meet you."

Marie picked that moment to begin crying in another room. Hub felt his heart jump in anticipation of seeing the baby, almost as if he'd forgotten her for a little while and suddenly remembered. "I'll get her...well, no, I guess I can't, Sarah. I'm too dirty."

"Never mind. There's water heating on the stove. Supper too. Clean up and we'll eat."

They carried the hot water to the barn and poured it into a number two tub, then used washcloths to scrub off most of the dirt. They hurried, because it was cold in the barn and because they still didn't know why the Indians had come. John's teeth chattered as he toweled himself dry and slipped into the clean clothing Hub had loaned him. He said, "Maybe this has something to do with Rock's dream."

Hub didn't answer. He'd been thinking about the mustang stallion, wondering if the horse was still around, asking himself again what he ought to do with the animal.

Sarah had the table set and carried Marie on her shoulder. She said, "You men sit down and eat. I'll go feed this girl."

They plowed into the venison steaks she'd fried, hungry enough to leave off conversation for a few minutes. It was Quanah Parker who broke the silence. "We'll be riding on pretty soon," he said, and took another bite of the meat. He chewed it slowly, swallowed and told them the story of his visit.

Hub caught Rock's eye and said, "I'm sorry. Real sorry." The Indian nodded.

Quanah went on, "We came by here because I wanted to see this young man for myself. We're much the same, you know. Both half-breeds, both standing in the middle of two worlds. But I see your father in your face, and that's what I most wanted to see. He lives in you."

"Most of my life I didn't even know about him."

"I understand. But now you do, and it makes you strong."

"My wife will have a baby soon."

"I saw your wife. A beautiful woman. Two Hawks will have a grandchild. This is good. Very good."

Hub said, "You don't have any trouble when you're off the reservation like this?"

"Sometimes I do. There are white men who'd like to kill me, many who've threatened it. But I dress in white clothing,

I mind my business, I carry a letter from the agency that says I have permission to travel."

"So you'll be protection for Rock on the way up there, but he'll be on his own coming back."

"Ben Turner wrote out a paper saying Falling Rock works for him and asking for his safe passage. I don't think he'll run into trouble."

"Would it help if I write out a paper, too?"

"Wouldn't hurt. Why don't you do that?"

Hub got up to find a sheet of paper and Sarah came back to the table holding Marie. John took her away and began walking the floor, singing the Comanche lullaby he had learned.

The two Indians stayed for half an hour after they'd eaten, Quanah full of talk, Falling Rock silent as always, his eyes cast down, sorrow evident in the lines of his body. Sarah said, "You're welcome to stay the night and leave in the morning."

"Oh, no, we can make good time tonight. I like to travel at night. It's one of the ways I stay out of trouble."

When they mounted up, stars already turning on to light the way, Quanah reached in a pocket and came out with something in his hand. "This is a gift for you, John. When my band was running from the soldiers I wasn't sure what we ought to do. I was standing up in a very high place praying for help and a wolf came and howled at me and an eagle flew over my head. It was plain to me what they said, and after that I led everyone to the reservation and started working for peace.

"This rock," he handed John a round stone, "is one I picked up at that place. I think where I stood was sacred and so the rock must be, too."

The stone was warm in John's hand. He tried to find words

of reply, but his throat became tight and unreliable, and he could only manage, "Thank you."

Even after the riders disappeared into the darkness the sound of their passage came back to the three who stood there— the scrape of a hoof, a muffled word, and then no sound at all. Hub held the baby wrapped against the cold night.

Sarah said, "He never took a warrior name."

John said, "What do you mean?"

"Quanah is his baby name, one his mother gave him. When he becomes a man a warrior takes another name, but Quanah never did because it came from her."

"Does it mean something in English?"

"It means fragrant."

CHAPTER 44

THE dun stallion and Mendoza's horse and the mule stood dozing inside the copse of trees where they had become accustomed to spending their nights. The noise of the two riders didn't spook the stallion. He was used to the presence of men now, and the night felt safe around him. Their scents, though, were the scents of the Indians who used to chase him and his mares over the prairie, trying to pen them, trying to catch them with nooses at the end of long poles, their whoops and yells ringing over the land, ringing above the frantic squeals of those they caught. There was quick rage at the smell of the men, but it burned away quickly and instead he remembered the mesa, the tall flat rock he loved to climb, the prairie around it, the fresh water of the springs.

For a long time after they hurt him and took him away from his place, the place he remembered now, it hadn't come into his mind; his thoughts filled always with fears and uncertainties and the need to do as men wished in order to avoid pain.

He took a forward step.

Nothing stood between this place and the other that had come like a dream just now into his thoughts. No man threatened him, no fence stretched across the land.

Another step. A murmur in his throat. His companions ignored him.

Slowly at first and then a little faster he began to walk, the scent trail of the two Indians and their ponies strong in his nose, the night growing cold. Where was the mare? It didn't matter. He couldn't force her, couldn't chase after her because of the pain in his leg and the shadow in his eye.

He walked on that way half the night, staying far behind the people, each step tentative, as though he might at any moment turn back, and then they stopped at a river and built a fire. He circled far to the north, swam across it and passed them by. Landmarks that he recognized, silhouetted shapes of black against the night sky, had begun appearing, and the remembrance of this path was strong in his heart, causing his breath to come deeper, causing him to push on.

Daylight came and still he walked in the northwest direction, led by markers he had used all his life—trees, rocks, gullies, hidden springs of water, all known, all remembered. More remembered now. Then, with the sun well up and the day bright he saw at last the thing he had imagined all night long with every step—the high mesa in the far distance, waiting as it had always waited, its colors like a taste on his tongue.

Another hour of walking and he was close enough to know this was where he belonged, and he looked around at the empty prairie. He had no manada, no companion, was alone under the sky. For a long time he stood there and looked at it, turned around twice in his tracks to see it all, and it came back then; everything came back—himself, his presence on this earth unfettered, unbounded by anything or anyone, hard and willful, demanding and bold. It came back.

He reared once for the joy of it. He was home.

* * *

Isidro had been awake for hours when morning came at last. The thoughts in his head had taken on long, dark shapes to match the night outside, and they were dry as sticks of wood, rattling around inside him, never coming to rest. All right, then. It's what he would do, because lying in this bed had become unbearable.

When the doctor came, as he did every morning, he looked a little worried and said, "Fever again. How do you feel?"

Felipe watched them from the other side of the room. Isidro said, "I feel pretty good, and Doctor, I want to talk to you man to man, not doctor to sick man."

"What's on your mind?"

"I want to leave."

"That's a bad idea. I can't allow it."

"That's what I mean about man to man, see? You have to allow it, because I am going to do it."

"Well, you've surprised me. Where would you go? If you left here?"

"Ain't sure about that, but I'm real sure about the leaving part. It's time for me to get out of this bed and out of this town."

"You will very likely kill yourself if you do it. I can't force you to stay, though, if you really don't want to. How do you plan to travel?"

"Don't worry about that. Felipe will help me."

"You have a horse, I believe, still out at the Anderson ranch."

"Yes, but Felipe will help me. I'll send the money to pay you when I can."

"No worry there. Mrs. Duncan took care of everything for you and her brother, as well. But I'll say again, I wish you would change your mind about this. Nothing good can come of it."

"It might. Maybe I'll see Estrella's face again."

"I suppose that could be a good thing. It's something I wish for myself, too."

"See? Not everything is bad."

The doctor left the room and when he was gone Isidro got himself upright and put his feet on the floor. There was not as much pain as he'd expected. He said to Felipe, "Would you kindly hand me my pants, please?"

"He said you still have a fever."

"That's nothing. It comes and goes." He felt dizzy standing up, but held Felipe's arm and stuck his feet into the trouser legs, then pulled them up and sat back down on the edge of the bed. "I have a great favor to ask you."

"Yes?"

"You know where is the place that has my horse and saddle. I need you to take me there."

"But how will I take you? Can you walk? It's a long way."

"No, I can't walk, but your legs are strong. You can carry me on your back if you will do it."

"Isidro, you know I have given up that way of thinking. I am not a horse."

"No, but you are my good friend with strong legs. Will you do it?"

It took time to convince him, not because he was unwilling to help, but because he was afraid of the things that might happen to them. In the end, though, he agreed, as Isidro had known he would.

They sat with Kountz at his breakfast table, the doctor watching Isidro intently all the time, noting his lack of appetite and the weakness of his voice. He'd bandaged the wound anew, offered to take him somewhere in his carriage, handed out warnings and at last had given up trying to change the man's mind.

Outside his door he helped Isidro onto Felipe's back then helped him lock his legs around the young man's waist to keep from falling off, noting the quickly hidden signs of pain on the pale face. And when Felipe began walking away with his burden Kountz called out, "You're trading your life for something. I wish I knew what it was."

"I already told you. Didn't you listen?"

CHAPTER 45

HUB had gotten his day started late. John had stayed after breakfast, in no hurry to head back to the Bent T, enjoying his mother and the baby. It had seemed good to Hub, as well, lingering at the table, talking as they had, the smells of coffee and food and the remembrance of the night before, the surprise they'd felt at finding the last Comanche war chief waiting for them. The morning had been good.

He'd stayed true to his word last night, and gone back to curry the mare and turn her out to pasture before he put his own tired body to bed. This morning he watched the horizon and wondered when they'd have their first blue norther. Couldn't be much longer now. He walked on, looking for the horses, carrying the mare's halter.

The three animals grazed together not far from the copse of trees where they'd spent the night. The stallion wasn't with them. Hub circled for a few minutes and saw no sign of him. Maybe he'd headed back to the mesa. It worried Hub. He'd been of two minds about keeping the horse all along, branding him, making him ranch property, protecting him; but the other way of thinking was opposed to that and made it feel wrong. Now it looked like the little dun had gone back to his wild ways, ways that would most probably mean his death before long. What should he have done?

"I don't know," Hub said, answering his own silent

question, slapping a hand across his leg, the noise sudden in the quiet morning, causing the grazing animals to raise their heads and stare at him.

As he went to get the mare a distant movement captured his attention, a horse trotting out of the treeline, and he thought for a second that the stallion hadn't gone after all, but there was a rider aboard, and it wasn't the stallion but a large sorrel that came on steady, and when the distance closed more he recognized the man—it was the young cowboy Elmo from the Duncan ranch.

"Morning, Mr. Anderson." He took off his hat and hung it on the saddle horn. His hair was stuck against his head like a blond cap.

Hub looked at the line of trees. No more riders. Looked like the man had come alone. "What can I do for you?"

Elmo reached into a hip pocket and brought out something folded. "Mr. Duncan sent this here money to you, on account of him accidentally shooting that dun horse of yours. It's two hundred dollars. That about right?"

"Duncan's the one shot him. Why didn't he bring the money?"

"Yes sir, I see what you mean, and maybe he would have, but him and his wife's gone off to Mexico on a horse buying trip, to replace his black. The one the mustang killed."

"When he comes back, tell him I'll take the two hundred when he brings it himself along with an apology."

Elmo grinned and slapped the money against the palm of his other hand, shook his head. "Mr. Anderson, I'll tell you the truth. Waitin' on Robert Duncan to apologize will be like waitin' on the second coming. It ain't apt to happen anytime soon."

"You tell him anyway."

"Yes sir, I guess you don't leave me no choice. I don't know when they're comin' back."

"I can wait. Tell him what I said."

"You bet I will. And say, have you seen hide nor hair of that mustang around here?"

"Nope. I guess he took off for different country."

"Yeah. I expect we're in for a long chase when the boss comes home." He stuck the money back in his pocket, put his hat on and laid the reins against the big horse's neck. "Good day to you."

Hub watched the man ride off, thinking about the money, and he decided not to tell Sarah. It would only make her mad that he'd refused it. They could use the cash, all right, and it was his stubborn pride that had gotten in the way again, a fact she would be quick to point out. He put the halter on the mare and led her toward the barn.

* * *

Charlie Boone and Raiford Clawson got the poles set for the inside of the barn, poles that would carry the weight of crossbeams and hold up the roof when it was put on. Tom hadn't come outside to help this morning. He hadn't felt good at breakfast and Charlie figured to let him be for a day, let him rest and maybe get over the melancholy the boy seemed to be feeling.

Clawson was a good worker and Charlie was trying his best to lighten up on the man, but he just couldn't seem to get over being mad. Who could, coming in behind a bunch of fools and trying to mend what they'd done? And McGee—not one word of regret. Dead dogs, burned barn, cut fence and not a word.

The two worked through the morning til Rose rang her bell and they washed up and went inside to eat. The boy was still in bed.

Charlie said, "Tom coming to eat?"

"I don't think so."

He got up from his chair and went into his son's room. "Don't you want some of your mama's cookin'?"

No answer from the bed. He walked over and pulled the covers back and the look on Tom's face, the tears, the fear, was almost enough to bring Charlie to his knees. "Son, what's the matter? What's tearing you up thisaway?"

He got nothing in return but a shake of the head.

"Well now, you got to tell me something. I can't just walk back out and go to eating with you in this shape. You tell me. What's the matter with you?"

"I'm scared, Daddy. I want to leave here."

"That's the thing makin' you sick? Got you cryin' in your bed?"

"I'm a coward, Daddy. I didn't do nothing to stop all that stuff. I was too scared. Can't we just go away?"

"No, son, we can't. And you ain't no coward, neither, and don't be thinking you are. You just a boy, and you wasn't no more scared than your daddy. You rest and don't be cryin' no more. There ain't nothing for you to be afraid of. I'm about to fix it."

Charlie got his pistol and loaded it, strapped the belt on and went through the kitchen and out the back door.

"Charlie Boone? Where you headed with that gun?" Rosabelle was after him in a few seconds, but he had already reached his unsaddled horse and was fumbling the bridle bit into the cowpony's mouth. He threw a leg over and pulled himself up. The horse danced in a circle, startled by the sudden weight on his bare back.

"Talk to me, Charlie. Don't you go off and do something crazy, now!"

"I'm sorry, Rosabelle." He put both heels in the horse's flanks and she was left standing there alone. It wasn't clear to her what he was sorry for.

"I reckon he's headed for the McGee place," Raiford said behind her.

She didn't trust herself to speak, it had all been so quick to happen, and she felt so very afraid.

"He ain't going to want my interference, either."

She managed to say, "I got no right to ask you, but follow him, won't you please? I can't stand to lose him. Can't stand it."

There was no way Raiford was riding that distance bareback, so Charlie got a good start on him while he rounded up his rig, saddled his own horse and made his way off the place and struck a trot in the direction of the McGee ranch. He was reluctant to go, knowing Charlie would resent him coming, but the woman was nearly crazy with worry and had seemed a little comforted when he told her he would go and help if he could.

CHAPTER 46

I T was the middle of the afternoon when Ivy finally finished up with the feeding and cleaning of the old man. Young Mr. William was dressed like he intended going out to work, but he didn't do a thing except sit in his bedroom just like the day before. She didn't think he was hurt all that bad, except for his pride, and she dared not say a word to him because it was her own shameful fault and he was never going to let her forget it. Maybe she'd been a fool to come back here, but when she'd fired off that gun in her moment of anguish and caused the poor boy to be hurt, she had realized in the very same moment that she could have no life apart from him. She sighed over that fact, and wondered again at herself.

Now what was that outside? Sounded like somebody yelling.

When she opened the door there sat Charlie astride his horse not a half dozen paces away. His voice when he spoke was no longer loud. It came out in a whisper she had to lean outside to hear.

"Tell Mr. William to get out here."

"What you thinking? You ain't going to hurt him, no sir."

William McGee limped past her in the doorway, using the walking stick Charlie had cut for him, and for which he had neither felt nor spoken any word of gratitude.

"Go inside, Ivy. I'll take care of this."

Charlie slid to the ground and slapped his horse on the rump. It ran to the edge of the yard and started to crop grass. Charlie backed away until he was separated from William by at least twenty paces, maybe a few more.

"You bring a gun McGee?"

"Mr. McGee to you."

Charlie drew his own pistol and let it hang beside his leg. He said again, "You bring a gun with you McGee?"

The little man drew back his coat to show the full holster on his hip.

"That's good." He backed up another ten paces. "Now you go on and pull that thing and see if you can shoot yourself a darkie!"

From somewhere inside the house Ivy called out, "Don't do it, Mr. William. Come back in here."

There were three or four men moving around far behind the house where the old barn was torn down, but they either didn't notice or didn't care what was happening.

William said, "You'll fire if I draw my gun."

"Oh, no. You wrong again. I want you to have your chance, McGee, you been so hot after me. You done caught me now, so shoot. After you miss me— and you are gonna miss me because your hand is shaking—after you miss me I am going to shoot you dead right where you stand."

William wore a sick look on his face that turned resolute. Ivy came out the door to stand beside him.

"You go home now, Charlie. This man is hurt and he ain't in no shape to fight you."

"His gun hand's okay. Nothing wrong with it." He waited and watched the resolution fade and fear take its place. "I'm giving you no choice. You shoot or I will, and I won't miss."

With a sudden jerk of his shoulder, William had the butt of his revolver in his hand and was swinging it up when the woman threw herself in front of him screaming, "No!"

The barrel couldn't have been more than an inch or two from her chest when the explosion came, the force of it propelling her backward, her feet and legs working at the ground. But the life they'd carried, the life of a faithful and decent woman, had already gone. She collapsed face-up, arms spread wide, staring at a small cloud drifting past overhead.

Raiford watched it all from the shadows, sitting his horse a few feet back in the trees, close enough to know what had happened. His rifle lay across the pommel of his saddle, but in truth he had not known what he ought to do. It had been plain that Charlie intended forcing a fight, but no matter what Rosabelle had wanted, how afraid she'd been, this was nothing he ought to enter into. Raiford's rifle might save the man's life, all right, but Charlie would never thank him for it.

Little McGee dropped the pistol and went down on his knees in a gesture that might have been sorrow, but in reality was an attempt to evade the bullet he thought was coming. Raiford watched Charlie holster his weapon and walk slowly toward the place where Ivy lay, and his harsh words came clearly to Raiford, already turning his horse away.

"Looks like you killed yourself another darkie, McGee."

CHAPTER 47

THE Duncans made quick time to the border. Robert had, bit by bit, given up cooperation, conversation and forgiveness. He had driven the horses hard, dark-faced and rigid in his carriage seat. After a day of it Estrella had retreated into her own silence, regretting that she'd come, wishing she hadn't talked him into the trip. By the time they left Del Rio and crossed the Rio Grande into Ciudad Acuña she only wished to conclude their business and return home.

"What is the name of this horse ranch? I forgot to ask."

"Soledad. Rancho Soledad."

"Ah, a lonely place, I take it. Solitude."

"Once, but not any more, I imagine It's a very big rancho."

"And where is the headquarters?" Strange how Robert could speak with such ease and gentleness and not feel those things at all.

"I don't know. When I came I was a little girl. It is by the river, I remember."

Acuña was not very large, not at all what Robert had imagined. Just a collection of adobe buildings, many whose walls were broken, whose ceilings were fallen. In the maze of dusty streets skinny men under dirty sombreros walked beside donkeys loaded with burdens. The air was heavy with the smells of grease and cooking meat and wood smoke. The thin sound of a guitar filtered from somewhere.

"I'll stop the carriage beside that donkey driver up ahead of us. Why don't you ask directions?"

The man was old and seemed hard of hearing, but she repeated questions until he understood what she was asking. He relaxed into a pleased grin around broken teeth and began to nod his head and point, and told her what they should do. Estrella found her purse and gave him a coin. The old man held it in one hand and slowly removed his sombrero with the other. He attempted to say something, but the carriage moved away and left him standing there with his donkey and his new coin and a shine in his eyes as if he had just observed a miracle.

"What did he say?"

"Drive on. I'll tell you when we come to the turn."

Two miles south of the village she showed him the turnoff, and there was in fact a rough wooden sign with an arrow and a few letters done with black paint, long ago faded to near the color of the wood—SOLIDAD.

They continued for the better part of an hour without seeing more than an occasional adobe hut with trash piled close by and small herds of Spanish goats that looked, despite the overgrazed countryside, healthy and well-fed.

Robert said, "Those animals must live on prickly pear."

"Yes, I think they do."

"This is a sorry looking place we've come, my dear. I begin to doubt we'll find a horse worth the trip."

"Be patient, Robert. I'm sure we will." But she was not at all sure, and her husband was probably right. How silly she'd been to lure him on this goose chase.

A dozen cattle blocked the road and showed no sign of moving out of the way. The animals watched them with disinterested eyes as Robert stood up in the carriage and popped his whip in the air, yelling threats. At last he took his seat and guided the team out of the sandy ruts they'd been following and through the low brush surrounding them, then back onto the road on the other side of the stubborn bunch.

The Rio Grande showed itself to the distant north with glistening, scattered winks through stands of mesquite trees and low desert vegetation. He said, "I suppose they're on their way to water."

"Yes, and stopped for the siesta." Her comment made him smile, but she had no faith in the smile.

Around the next bend the trail ran closer to the river, and cottonwoods, with their roots sunk deep after water, lined the bank. In their shade were horses—not many; Estrella counted only ten mares, all branded as the cattle had been with the simple S of the ranch. There were buildings ahead, an entrance of sorts built of stacked stones and then a rail fence on either side of the trail leading away from the river to higher ground.

The buildings were all adobe structures, flat-roofed with no flash of color anywhere, everything erected for utility, dull and hard, as if centuries had weighed them down and compressed them into the least possible space. The air carried the smells of animal waste, the constant droppings of the years—a place of hoofs and hard living.

"I remember it," Estrella said, "it hasn't changed."

CHAPTER 48

FIGURES on foot and on horseback were in motion up ahead, something happening in a corral two hundred yards distant.

"I wonder where the main house is, or the office. Is there one?"

"I'm sorry, but I don't remember about that. I can ask someone."

"We'll go over to that corral. It seems to be the center of activity."

Another carriage stood at a hitch rail not far from the corral and he drove the team there and tied them to the cedar rail that had probably been cut a hundred years before. It was polished to a shiny smoothness by use. He helped Estrella down from the carriage and they started toward the corral as a single man separated himself from a small group in the shade of a live oak and came to meet them.

The man was tall and very thin. He looked the color and consistency of hard, dry leather, his boots the color of adobe, his clothing thick and rough against the brush and thorns of the countryside. The sombrero he wore was stained with sweat, dark with the leavings of wind and hand. He removed it and revealed a face that would have been austere without the wide smile. He rattled off something in Spanish to Estrella, and nodded at her answer. He spoke to Robert in accented English, offering a handshake.

"Good afternoon, Señor. My name is Lalo Barron. I'm the boss on Soledad."

Robert shook the extended hand and matched Barron's smile. "Robert Duncan, pleased to know you. My wife, Mrs. Duncan." Barron directed a brief nod of his head to Estrella. Robert went on, "I've come seeking a horse. A stallion."

Barron gestured toward the corral. "Today I'm delivering a remuda of mares and geldings to that ranchman over there. In a little while the men will drive them away and I can talk to you more. Come and watch, if you like."

"You said you're the boss. I intend no offence, but are you the owner? I'd prefer to deal with the owner."

The grin stayed in place. "I would like that myself sometimes, Señor. There are many owners, but not one who will talk to you about a stallion. They are in Mexico City, Guadalajara, other places, drinking French wine and watching bullfights."

"Stockholders."

"Si." He replaced his sombrero.

"How large is this ranch?"

"Much of it has been sold off in the past fifteen years, but we stock 20,000 hectares now, nearly 50,000 acres."

"A great deal of land."

"Yes, certainly, but it is desert country. Never much grass."

"Do you feed your stock? Your horses, I mean."

"Si, horses and cattle, too. We tap the river for irrigation and plant fields of corn and oats. This the ranch has always done, long before me."

"So your animals should be in good condition."

"You'll see. Come along."

Walking toward the cluster of men in the shade Estrella opened her mind to memories of the time her father had brought her to this same ground, but there was little to remember—his large hand holding hers, guiding her, protecting her as always, standing in conversation beneath a tree, probably this very one, the surge of frightened animals, the long ride home. She felt a longing for that time as though it were a shelter she might run to.

Through the rails she could see the herd of horses milling about in silence, looking for a way out of the pen, their eyes wide and white with fear of the unknown.

Barron began instructing his men in rapid Spanish. All but one were Mexican vaqueros, dark men of the brush country, thin as whips, who threw down their cigarettes and headed for the corral to hobble the bunch as Barron had instructed. The man remaining she knew belonged to the buggy, a short man running to weight in a dusty suit of clothing. His face was half hidden by a close-cut beard turned nearly white.

Still in Spanish the foreman said to her, "Forgive me, but your name has abandoned me. Duncan?" She nodded and he went on, "Señor Vasquez, Mr. And Mrs. Duncan, come from El Norte to buy a stallion."

Vasquez took off his hat and gave her a slight bow, then reached to shake Robert's hand as Barron said, "Señor Vasquez has no English. He's the buyer of this remuda for his own hacienda three day's ride east of here."

To Estrella, Vasquez said in words Robert couldn't understand, "If it's a stallion you want, don't fail to see the white Andalusian."

"What's he saying?" Robert wanted to know. Estrella had always thought it strange that Robert, while professing to love her, despised the language of her birth. She told him what the old rancher had said.

Barron said, "The stallion he speaks of we can see today if you want. But now you are tired and hungry. I'll show you a room where buyers stay sometimes, where you can rest a little, and if you want to eat I'll have our cook make you something."

CHAPTER 49

RAIFORD Clawson kept his horse at a trot. Charlie would be a while coming home, but Raiford was not going to mess in that business back there. Too bad the woman had died, and it hadn't been about saving Boone, either—she went down trying to keep that little Mississippi dude from taking a bullet, because like Charlie had said, William would have missed his shot, and that's how it would have played out. Charlie would've killed the man, and after that it was anybody's guess just how it all would end.

Too much trouble and pain. He was tired of it. He would carry the news to Rosabelle. She deserved to know her husband was all right, but come morning he was through with barn building for a while. He had done wrong, like the other men involved, and he had tried to make amends. But tomorrow he intended heading for town and enough whiskey to wash away the taste of good deeds. Maybe have a little visit with Jezzie. Maybe a little visit with the sheriff.

Hub had spent the afternoon thinning out a stand of thorn, piled it and burned it down to ash and stayed with it to be sure there were no live coals to spark another blaze. Smoke from the fire was in his clothes and hair. What had at first been a pleasant scent in the cool afternoon had become something he wanted rid of now, riding home with the idea of soap and warm water and clean clothes on his mind.

Before he was in sight of the house Sarah came walking toward him with Marie on her shoulder, picking her way through the brown grass, waving at him from a distance then waiting while he came closer.

She was something to see, Sarah was, with that long blonde hair and pretty face, and he marveled again at the life he'd been given when so many—his own brother among them—had never made it past the battlefields.

"You girls out for your exercise?"

She didn't smile. "Those men are back here."

"What men, Sarah?"

"The Duncan woman's brother and the other one—the wounded man I doctored."

He got down and took Marie, helped Sarah mount up then pulled himself and the baby onto the mare's rump behind the saddle.

"Well, that gut-shot feller can't be well yet. I thought he was at the doctor's, in town."

"He's not well. He's unconscious and I think he's dying. The brother hasn't got anything much to say, just sort of stands around."

"Where are they now?"

She didn't answer.

"Sarah?"

"I put him in our bed, Hub."

He only sighed at the news and touched the mare's flank with a boot heel. A few minutes later he unsaddled her and left her in the corral with a few ears of husked corn then went in the house.

"You both walked here?" He put the question to Felipe and got a shake of the man's head.

"I carried him."

"All the way from town?"

"It's what he wanted."

"And Doctor Kountz didn't stop him?"

Felipe seemed embarrassed. "Yes, he tried, but...I think Isidro will die. He thinks so, too. He wants to see my sister again before...he loved her you see, all his life. If you will let him stay for a little I can go and tell her he's here at your house."

Hub shook his head. "Your sister is gone to Mexico."

"How do you know that?"

"One of their riders." He glanced at Sarah, busy in the kitchen. "Said she went with her husband to buy a horse."

Felipe considered the news. "It's too much to ask for myself, but for Isidro who is dying, will you let him stay until I can find her?"

Hub took in a deep breath and blew it out. "Well, I'm not throwing him out in the yard, the shape he's in, so yeah, I guess he can. And you, too. She ought to be home in a few days."

"The wild stallion is not close by." It was not a question.

"No, he's gone off. I figure he went back home."

CHAPTER 50

THE ranch cook was an old Mexican woman who spoke no English and didn't need to. Estrella tried to begin conversation with her as they ate in the kitchen of the main house, and the woman would answer her direct questions, but made no effort to add anything more, so Estrella gave up and ate her food in silence as Robert did. The old woman served them beef stew left over from the midday meal, with fresh tortillas and some kind of sweet pastry for dessert. When Lalo Barron came for them Estrella was feeling rested and much stronger.

They left headquarters in a rough wagon pulled by two mules, the wagon bed partially filled with shelled corn. Barron drove the team and Estrella sat on the seat beside him. Robert knelt on the bare wood behind them, his knees cushioned by empty sacks Barron had tossed to him.

"We feed when it's needed," Barron said. "Everything is pretty fat right now, but this will bring horses when I put it out. Maybe that Andalusian will be one of them, maybe not. We got a lot of fine animals. He is one, but there's plenty more."

Robert said, "I'm only interested in stallions."

Barron was silent for a few moments and said, "Yes, I know that. I don't keep as many as I used to. They fight, you know, steal mares back and forth, keeps 'em skinny and bloody. We fix most of them now, pretty early. But the Andalusian is one, and there's three or four more that we can look at on this trip."

Estrella could see bits of silver come and go in the distance, the Rio Grande in its eastward flow, or the Rio Bravo, as Mexicans called it. They made slow time over land that gave off a smell like the closed-up rooms in old houses. The air about them seemed to sit on the sparse grass as if it were too tired to move. Barron stopped the team beside a long, rectangular trough built with thick boards. It had been there a long time, without a roof of any sort to shelter it from sun and rain. No shade cooled it, the closest trees hundreds of yards away. The wood of the trough was gray with age, warped, rubbed smooth by tongues and muzzles, the edges along the top rounded by use. The soil around it was compacted and hard. No grass or weed could grow in it. Probably no drop of rain could penetrate it. The trough had very likely been right here in this spot, looking just like this, gray and warped, during her long ago visit.

Barron used a wide shovel to remove some of the corn from the wagon bed, sliding the shovel under the yellow kernels and lifting them out in heavy loads that made him grunt as he threw them through the air with practiced aim, most of it falling into the trough and raising clouds of white dust, other bits of yellow catching on the edges or missing the target altogether and falling to the ground. The corn and the dust it raised smelled to her like corncribs she had once loved to play in, moving about on scuffed knees over dried, noisy, scratchy husks. Barron called out as he shoveled, with a high, wordless keen that seemed sharp enough to cut its way through rock, and in seconds animals appeared from the distant trees, their raised heads and eyes showing above the tops of little hills, all moving here, answering the call.

Robert had climbed out of the wagon and stood brushing at his trousers. She heard him say, "That is the stallion?"

"Yes, the rest are mares and geldings. He keeps them together for me."

Estrella, too, climbed down and watched the approach of the horses. This was something they were used to—none showed any reluctance. The feed was a powerful draw. As she had expected, the stallion was solid white. He was tall, with dark hoofs, and his tail and mane were long and ungroomed, a little darker than his coat, ivory in color, perhaps, and shining like silk. His face was well-formed, eyes large and intelligent.

"What a beautiful animal," Robert said.

The horses paid them little mind, crowding around the trough, standing side by side and shoving their muzzles into the corn, coming up with bits of it dripping from their lips as they chewed. All the animals appeared healthy and well-fed.

Barron pulled a rope halter from under the wagon seat and walked toward the stallion. "You see how polite he is? He lets the others eat first while he watches for danger. Not all stallions are so sweet, you know." The big white allowed Barron to slide the halter over his nose. "Look him over, Mr. Duncan. He's very sound, you'll see."

"Yes, yes, I have no doubt." Robert circled the quiet horse, looked at his feet, his teeth. "Do you have lineage records on him?"

"Yes. Back for a long way. The Andalusian is the oldest of all the breeds, did you know that?"

"As a matter of fact, I do. They came into being on the Iberian Peninsula, came to America with Cortez. This is a warhorse, you know. My people, the English, rode them in the crusades. Quite an ancestry."

"Try him out if you'd like. He'll answer to the halter. Here, I'll help you up."

Robert mounted with an assist from Barron's clasped hands and rode the stallion away from them for a short distance, then swung him in a circle and came back. He slid to the ground and dropped the rope, then walked away.

"You see? He remains in place. He is very well trained."

"Yes. Can we see some others before dark?"

As they rode away in the wagon over the rough ground, almost out of sight of the feed trough, Estrella watched the big white horse find himself a place and begin to eat. So, they would look at other horses, Robert would examine feet and teeth, but she knew from the shine in her husband's eyes that he would come back for this one.

CHAPTER 51

RAIFORD Clawson had continued driving nails when Charlie rode his quarter horse up to the house. He had come in two or three hours after Raiford's arrival, and the woman had been pacing outside, then inside, then out again as she worried over the news Raiford had brought her. They argued—he could hear their raised voices but couldn't make out the words, didn't want to make out the words, didn't want to be part of these troubles. A few minutes after it got quiet in there Charlie came out and took the bridle off his horse and turned him loose. Raiford kept on hammering.

"Ain't you hungry?"

"Reckon I am."

"Well, lay that hammer down. Things is all right. Rose'll have something on the table in a minute."

He hung the hammer on a nail driven into one of the upright posts. "I'm going into Junction City tonight or in the morning."

"Well, sure, that's your business."

"I mean, I ain't coming back out here. Not for a while, anyway."

"That's okay by me. You been a big help."

"I followed you out to McGee's."

"Yeah, I seen your tracks on the ride back. That's what we was fussing about just now. I appreciate you stayed out of it."

Raiford followed Charlie inside. Charlie turned to him and said, "If you wait til morning I'll go in with you. I want to tell the sheriff what happened. Wouldn't hurt none if you backed up my story, too."

As they tied up at the rail in front of the office, Ames Bradberry was walking from the cafe beside another man who wore black clothing with a white clerical collar under his chin. A toothpick stuck out from the sheriff's lips. Bradberry said to the other man as they got closer, "You take care of that, then, and I'll see what these folks want with me."

He pulled a keyring out of his hip pocket and unlocked the door. "Deputy's gone to see about some land. I think he's a farmer at heart and don't care much for the lawman's life."

They followed him inside and he offered a handshake to each of them. To Raiford he said, "Don't believe we've met before."

Charlie took a chair and spoke up while the sheriff hung his hat. "Some bad stuff going on out at my place. Thought we better come tell you about it."

"More from the McGee bunch?"

Charlie told him what had happened.

"Y'all ought to've let me know in time. I could've stopped it and you'd still have your barn."

"Yes, sir, looking back I reckon I ought to've done that."

"And you didn't tell me all of it either, Charlie. I been in this business long enough to know how people think. I bet you had some help lined up to teach the man a lesson and things just didn't work out."

"Little bit of that, too, Sheriff."

"Mister Clawson, you have a familiar name. Is it your sister runs that little shop down the street?"

"Jezzie, that's right."

"And you witnessed it? When the woman got shot?"

"I was pretty close. It was plain what happened. McGee was about to shoot at Charlie and she just flung herself in front of the gun."

"Well, Charlie, I never thought you'd embark on such a foolish mission. If she hadn't done it, and he'd of killed you, what would happen to your family now? And if he'd shot and missed, what would you have done? Would you have shot to kill?"

"I don't know, Sheriff." He shook his head and looked at the floor. "My boy was at home crying and scared after what they done to us. I don't know. I was out of my head, I guess you could say."

"What about you, Mr. Clawson? You was one of the barn burners?"

"I was on the man's payroll, Sheriff, but I was not in on that. I never was clear on just what was about to happen or I never would've been there in the first place."

Charlie said, "I think he's being truthful about that. He seen to it I got that lumber and he's been at my house working on rebuilding the barn. McGee fired him because he didn't go along with it."

Bradberry played with a matchbox on his desk top, shoving it back and forth, shaking his head. "Reckon I'll go see McGee, see what he has to say. Not today, though. Charlie, go on home. We'll find a way through this mess. I doubt you have to worry about the little man again. Mr. Clawson, you plan to be in town a while?"

Raiford nodded.

"We got a session planned this morning at the courthouse and I believe I'd like your attendance."

CHAPTER 52

J AMES Harper saw the man come in the door. He knew the Methodist preacher by sight and reputation, though he'd never attended the small white church on the southern edge of town. "Haven't seen you for a while, Reverend Nelson."

The man's smile was like clothing. He always wore it. "How busy are you, James?"

James looked around the store. "Not very. You're the only customer right now. Why?"

"You've been invited to a private conference over at the courthouse. They asked me to bring you."

"What are you talking about? Who asked you?"

"Well, it concerns Jezebel Clawson, and she would like for you to attend it."

"You're not making much sense."

"No, but you'll understand it by and by. As one of our hymns says."

James hesitated for a few seconds, sighed a long breath and wrote out a piece of paper, which he left on the counter in case a customer came along while he was gone.

Instead of taking the main steps into the courthouse they went around to the side and entered through an almost hidden doorway that took them into a short hall, then into a room with a table that was surrounded by chairs as well as half a dozen benches along the wall. The preacher sat down on one of the benches and James took one for himself.

A tall, skinny cowboy occupied another bench, and at the table was Sheriff Bradberry and Jezzie, along with Judge Matthew Potter, the only judge since the county was organized. Potter was a medium-high man who had lived his early years as a range hand and still carried the weathered look of an outdoor life. Next to him was the county prosecutor, Sean Kennedy. Kennedy spoke with a bit of Irish in his voice, liked his whiskey and had the red face to prove it.

Potter spoke up. "Now this is not a regular session of the court. Everybody needs to understand that. Whatever is decided among us today, if anything, may not have any legal bearing at all. Got it?"

Silence in the room.

"Sheriff? You can go ahead."

Bradberry glanced around the room and said, "Thank you, Judge. Six or eight years ago, right ater the war, before this county was organized, when there was no law but a bunch of carpetbaggers and crooked police, this young lady did some things she wishes she hadn't of done. Things she wants to make right. There's no warrant out on her, no crime charged against her, and she understands that speaking out this way could bring that about.

"Anyway, Reverend Nelson come to see me a few days ago, tellin' me she spent some time with him getting his counsel, and this little meeting is the outcome. What I want to do, Judge, is let Miss Clawson tell the story in her own words, and then Mr. Kennedy can ask her any questions he wants to. You agreeable to that?"

"Well, I don't know. You a long-winded woman?"

Jezzie smiled. "No, sir. I am bluntly spoken as you will see."

"All right, then. But wait a minute—somebody get the clerk in here with a Bible."

They swore her in, hand on the black book. As she sat back down her eyes swept across James and he read in that instant the shyness on her face and thought he saw gratitude at his presence. So this is what it was all about—her reluctance, her need to make a decision. Not another man at all, but a moral question. She began.

"A troop of police was stationed here then, and Emil Dugan was its captain. I was his mistress." She paused over the word as though it pained her. James felt it, too. "He had declared martial law and he collected all sorts of taxes and fines from the people, and he kept the money in a safe in his office. I don't know exactly how much he had, but it was quite a lot. He was keeping it for himself, his own personal fortune. It wasn't money that was going to any government.

"So I decided to take it. I wrote a letter to my brother and he came here with two of his friends and they robbed the safe, took the money. One of the men, the youngest—I only heard the name Goose—shot one of the troopers. And one of the men with my brother was killed, too.

"I met them outside of town and the Goose fellow drew a gun on my brother. I killed him before he could shoot. He was a crazy little man. Then the two of us took the money and rode for California. We got away, we spent the money. I've come back here because I want to make a home. I want to settle down, and I've just lately realized that I want to set matters right over what I did then.

"This crime—I guess it was a crime, I know it was wrong whatever we call it—I want it off my conscience, and if I have to go to prison for it I'll serve my time without hard feelings. And when I've paid my debt I'll come back here, because I've decided this is home."

After a half minute of silence Judge Potter said, "Well, that's blunt enough, I reckon. Mr. Kennedy, you got anything to ask this lady?"

"Yes, your honor. Isn't it true you stole a horse from someone here in town?"

"No. I borrowed a horse and rode it to the point where I met up with my brother, but then I tied it beside the road and took another of the horses when we left."

"You took the horse of the young man you'd just killed?"

She was slow to answer that. "Yes."

"Did you ever stop to think about who that money really belonged to?"

"You mean the people around here, I guess. No, I didn't. I was as greedy then as the captain was, and I just wanted it, that's all. I didn't care. But I care now."

CHAPTER 53

THE preacher got to his feet. "Judge, if I may I'd like to offer a comment or two."

"I've heard your sermons, and I expect it'll be more like five or six comments, but go ahead."

"Your honor, Miss Clawson has experienced a profound change since the events she just described to you. I've been counseling her for some time, but she arrived at this conclusion on her own. She sincerely wants to live a new life, and I'm hopful that everybody involved with legal matters here will allow her to do it." He sat back down.

The judge said, "Sheriff Bradberry tells me this outlaw brother of yours is present today. Is he that vagabond over there?"

She glanced back at Raiford. "Yes, sir."

"If I was you, Mr. Clawson, I'd a been spurring hard for the border. Things she's said don't leave you in too good a light."

Raiford stood, holding his hat. His clothes were dusty and wrinkled, his beard untrimmed. "I was invited by the sheriff, Judge. I didn't think I could turn him down, and I didn't know what it was all about. I'm just now learning. But what Jezzie's told you is the truth. She shot Goose because he'd leveled down on me and would've killed me for sure He was a murderous boy. And I want to say I'm proud of you, Jezzie. It's time we both quit looking over our shoulders."

"All right, take your seat. Mr. Kennedy, you have a mind to file charges against either one right now?"

"Seems like there ought to be some, Judge, but I don't know just what. At the very least there ought to be a sizeable fine to pay back the people of this county."

"But was there any records? We know who paid into it? We know how much it was?"

"No, sir, to all your questions. No records were ever kept."

"So it could've been a sack of beans or a barrel of gold they stole and no way of knowing which. Whatever it was, they stole it from a man who stole it from somebody else. I don't believe I've come across a web so tangled. Have you?"

Kennedy said, "No, sir."

"How about you Ames? You want to throw either one in the clinker?"

The sheriff laughed. "Not today, Judge. It needs a good deal more studying."

Potter put his elbow on the table and leaned his head into his hand, rubbing his forehead as if he might encourage straight thought that way. The room was quiet. "Miss Clawson, you've brought some serious matters before me, and I want it clear that I take all of them seriously. Just now I don't know where it will lead, what sort of charges, if any, may be lodged against you, but rest assured I'll see justice done to the best of my ability. I don't see why you can't go on with your life til some conclusion is reached by the prosecutor. And the same goes for your brother back there on the bench. Both of you need to stay in the county til you hear different. You run off and Ames Bradberry, who is the best tracker and second-best horseshoe pitcher in the state will be after you. That clear?"

Jezzie said, "Yes, sir. Thank you."

"So now you've got it off your conscience and into our legal laps, you might say. Meeting over."

There was a general commotion as everybody stood, moving chairs and benches, talking to one another, the judge and prosecutor out the door and gone.

James hung back while most everybody filed out, hoping to talk to Jezzie, but the preacher went over to her and took her arm and they left together. He wandered into the empty hall thinking about it, how it felt to know there was no other man involved, weighing that against the things she'd admitted to. She'd wanted him here, wanted him to know the whole story. But then she'd scooted off with the Reverend without even a backward glance, and that had snuffed his excitement. He opened the door and stepped outside and headed for his store. Reverend Nelson was walking away alone and Raiford was with the sheriff. Jezzie had disappeared.

Her voice came from behind him. "Hey, James." He stopped to look back and saw her leaning against the court-house wall.

"What's your hurry?"

He couldn't get his throat to work.

She smiled at him and said, "I was thinking maybe we could go have some breakfast together."

CHAPTER 54

HUB didn't mind sleeping on the floor the first night, or even the second for that matter, but the situation was beginning to irritate him by the third morning.

"I got a mind to haul him back to town," he said to Sarah, biting into a biscuit and washing it down with coffee. The brother had already left the house for the day—he only came inside at night and sometimes to eat a little, preferring to roam the countryside alone, saying little, keeping whatever thoughts he had to himself.

"The trip would kill him."

"I know you're right, Sarah, but I'm at the end of my rope with these boys. I'm scared to go off working stock, no telling what'll happen while I'm gone."

"Lower your voice. He'll hear you."

He didn't lower his voice. "I don't care. Call me hard-hearted, but I never seen nobody take so long to cash in. It seems like everybody in the state's waiting on it to happen, but we're the ones get to sleep on a pallet while he goes about it."

"He won't live much longer. A day or two, I think. Anyway, I'm the one taking care of him. Go on and work your stock, I don't care."

Hub drank the last of his coffee and held out the empty cup for more.

"Get it yourself. I don't wait on hard-hearted men."

He didn't move. "I'm sorry. I didn't mean it, you know that. I feel sorry for the man, but I feel sorry for us, too."

"Get your own coffee, anyway." But she was smiling at him, and after a long enough time to make her point she took the cup from him and filled it and brought it back to the table.

Felipe came in the back door. "They will be home soon."

Hub turned to look at him. Sarah said, "Who? Your sister, you mean?"

"Yes. I'll go bring her."

Hub said, "What makes you think so?"

He shrugged. "I just know."

"I thought Duncan was after you for setting the mustang loose. You not afraid of him?"

"He'll be gone when I get there."

Sarah said, "Now you can't know that for sure."

"Oh, yes, he has a new horse to ride."

And he was out the door before either of them could say another word, running through the back pasture at an easy trot.

"Now tell me," Hub said, "if that ain't crazy. Like it come to him through the air."

"Maybe it did. Eat your food."

Isidro almost died that night. His fever burned high and he moaned with delirium, keeping them awake until near daylight. Sarah tried feeding him the potion she boiled out of willow bark, but he was never awake enough to swallow it. The skin around his eyes grew darker and his breath rattled.

Hub checked on Marie again and found her still asleep. That had been the only good thing about the night—the baby had slept clear through it. The odor of Isidro's worsening wound had spread all over the house.

"We'll have to buy new bedding," Hub said.

"No, we won't. I'll take care of it, you'll see."

"You know, Sarah, the man has been lucky in a way, to have you taking care of him. Even if he's about finished out he's in a warm bed, anyhow. And I'm a lucky man, too. There's not a woman anywhere like you. I don't say it enough, how special you are. To me, and to everybody."

She blushed and patted him on the arm in an absent-minded way. "You think they'll get here before...?"

"Don't know, hon. We'll just wait and see."

"Hello?" It was Isidro's voice from the bedroom, weak and surprising to hear.

Sarah went first, with a glass of the medicine. "Can you drink this? It may help the fever."

He took the glass and swallowed the contents. "Thank you. I felt very thirsty." His voice was strangely clear, his face composed, as though last night had never happened. "Is it your bed I'm in?"

"Yes," she said, "you've been very sick."

"My friend, Felipe—is he here?"

Hub said, "He went to fetch Mrs. Duncan."

"Oh, then maybe my prayer is answered."

Hub left the room and walked outside. The sun was halfway up on the eastern horizon. Hard to know what to think about the sick man. Seemed all night like any second could be his last and now here he was awake and asking questions. Hub didn't doubt that it was Robert Duncan put a bullet in him, left him to die on the prairie. Duncan had a lot to answer for. The morning air was sweet with grass and sun and the edge of chill that had settled in overnight.

Sarah joined him in a few minutes. "He's asleep again. Any sign of her?"

"No."

"He won't last the day out. Sometimes people get clear-headed just before they sink down and die, and I think that's what he's done. He's holding on to see her one more time."

"She's another man's wife."

"I think there's a whole lot to this story we don't know about."

"Well, let me ask a favor of you—if you find out, don't tell me."

She laughed. "You old grouch. You can't wait to hear it. I'll bet it's a dark scandal."

Felipe appeared just then around the side of the house. Behind him on her horse was Estrella Duncan. They had come by the road. Hub helped her down and tied the horse. She looked tired.

"We started after midnight. Is Isidro...?"

"He's alive," Sarah said. They went in the house, Felipe beside his sister, Hub bringing up the rear.

Estrella went to the bed and leaned over it, gazing down on Isidro. He looked terrible, Hub thought, with days of uncut whiskers on his face, a hollowed-out look to his flesh. The room was thick with the stink of him.

"Isidro?" She said. "Isidro? I'm here." There was no response and Hub thought maybe he was gone. The blanket lay still over the bony chest. But then a breath, a rise and fall, a sigh. "Open your eyes. Look at me."

But the eyes did not open. Estrella lowered her face to his and kissed him on the thin, dry lips. A little, then, the eyes opened—not much—and he smiled, the corners of his mouth turning up and causing the skin of his cheeks to wrinkle. And he nodded, just a little, just enough, and that was all.

Hub turned his back and was quick to leave the house. As he walked he cleared his throat and tried to blink away the sudden, unexpected blur of tears.

CHAPTER 55

GUS Meyer banged through the door and dropped the mail he was carrying onto Bradberry's desk.

"Stage come through?" I guess I wasn't paying attention, caught up like I was in conversation."

Raiford sat in the side chair at his desk, his hat on his lap and a worried look on his face.

"Yes, sir. If you don't need me for a while now I'd like to take some of the day off."

"Ain't found a good claim yet, Gustave?"

"No. What I want is a valley with enough dirt to plow."

"You ought to go east, then, over towards the Brazos or south down around San Antonio, if it's dirt you're looking for What we got here's rocks. And under them is more rocks."

"No, I don't want to leave here. Somewhere I'll find my spot."

"Go on, then. I wish you good luck."

When the deputy had gone Bradberry picked up the mail and sifted through it. "I don't see any wanted posters on you, so I guess you're safe for a while, anyhow." He opened a drawer and put the mail inside it, then lifted out a sheet of paper. "This here is a telegram that come from Walt McGee's daughter up in Long Island, New York. I felt like maybe her presence here would soothe the troubled waters.

"She's on her way, according to this. It'll take railroad,

steamboat and stagecoach, but she says she's coming, and mad as a bumblebee at cousin William for trying to take things over. When Clarice Davis gets here—that's how she signed the telegram—she will need the help and guidance of a man such as yourself to run that place. Think you can stay honest long enough to do it?"

"I can stay honest from here on out, Sheriff, but that don't mean she'll hire me."

"Well, maybe not, and anyway I'll have you trained for deputy by then."

"That'd be the day. A man that's spent his life breaking the law don't sound to me like deputy material."

"On the contrary. Many a badge is pinned on repentant badmen. The work's much the same. I'm riding out to McGee's in the morning with this news about the widow Davis and I'd like you to come along. Might be something you can clear up."

"Well, thanks for askin', but..."

"Now Raiford, what makes you think I was asking?"

                              * * *

Robert had spent the night at the spot where he shot Isidro Mendoza out of the saddle. Or part of the night anyway. When they had arrived home in the middle of the day he'd felt in a hurry to saddle and ride the Andalusian. He had put the same outfit on this one that he'd used for the black stallion. Later he'd have a new saddle made, but this one was fine for now, and it was a pleasure riding the new horse, tall and graceful and quickly obedient.

He'd made concession after concession to Estrella before leaving. He had sat with her at the table over a meal she cooked. They'd made do with beans and tortillas on the trip and the food from her kitchen was delicious. He'd told her so. She'd wanted to talk and he had tried joining her in conversation, but finally impatience had set in, a need to be in the saddle, riding across the prairie, and sometime near dark he had left her, tearful words or no. There were limits.

This would be a hunt, all right, but he carried a loaded rifle, not the falcon. He'd ridden much of the night to this place, but there was no sign of the bones he'd expected to find. And now in full daylight he searched again but saw nothing. What happened to the body? He'd left the man dying, there was no doubt at all. Wolves or coyotes must have carried off the bones after the vultures finished with it. He saddled the Andalusian and offered the bridle bit to the big horse, who dropped his head and continued grazing. Without hesitation Robert drove his fist into the ribs behind the saddle skirt. The horse grunted and lunged away. The Englishman walked over to where his new mount stood trembling and tried the bridle again and this time there was no problem at all.

CHAPTER 56

THE sun hung straight above the mesa. The mustang stallion had no mares to guard, but out of habit and out of desire he stood on top of the rose-hued rock and watched the prairie for danger as he had always done. He had gone early for water and grass and was comfortable there, the sun warm now, making his shadow puddle at his feet so that he seemed to step on it when he moved.

His leg still hurt and he'd not yet been able to round up another manada, but he pictured that he would, could see them as they would be soon, his to protect and govern. Going down and coming up the trail of rubble behind the mesa was made difficult by the leg and by his injured eye, and so he made few trips. Every day was like today—the land empty except for a wolf or an antelope, sometimes a pair of coyotes.

Movement caught his attention. He shifted his head to see from the good eye. A horse and rider far away but moving toward him. He stiffened with anticipation. But no, the sore leg would keep him from running. Already he could see that the horse was big and powerful and would be able to catch him. They came on and soon he recognized the rider—it was the man who had hurt him so badly, hurt his leg, made the shadow in his eye. Until this moment he had forgotten that man, but now pictures filled his mind of the beating and the terror he had endured, and in his heart rose a dark and unforgiving hatred.

Robert had come hoping to find some sign of the mustang, and this was almost too good to be true. There the animal stood in plain view on top of the rock. He rode closer and saw him back away from the edge as though to climb down the back side. For once he was sure that the horse he rode was capable of catching the wild one, so let him try to escape. But no, there he was at the edge again, stamping his foot as if he knew Robert and was throwing out a challenge. There was no herd of mares, no other horses anywhere around, just the single, lone dun.

"I'll make this quick, then." He rode right up to the sheer rock of the mesa's south face and dismounted, bringing the rifle out of its sheath. The Andalusian shied away when he turned loose of the reins, but he paid no attention.

He levered a round into place and raised the rifle barrel straight up, looking almost directly into the sun. The mustang was peering over the edge at him and it was a perfect shot, but before he could pull the trigger the dun eased back out of sight. Was he headed down the back way after all? Not likely. All that loose rock would have made plenty of noise, and there wasn't a sound to be heard.

"Come on," he said, holding the sights on the mesa edge, waiting, and then something happened between his eyes and the sun. A scream such as he had never heard before sliced the air, sharp and dark as an obsidian blade. The mustang had leapt off the rock directly above him and was falling faster than thought out of the ancient sky.

CHAPTER 57

SPRING came a couple of weeks early that year, and it was a wet one, too, so that trees were especially green and flowers seemed to be everywhere. The antelope and deer and ranch stock turned fat and sleek from the abundance.

And summer, too, seemed kinder to the land, so that it didn't dry away to dust in the heat. Settlers pushing west may have seen a southbound rider pulling a burden wrapped in canvas, suspended between two poles, as once the Indians had traveled, a sad man carrying the bones of his son out of an angry past to a place of rest.

Fall gave way to an early winter freeze that stole the green from the grass and dropped the leaves off cottonwoods, turning the hills red with sumac and Spanish oak again.

Doctor Kountz bundled himself against the cold and continued driving his buggy from Junction City out to the Duncan headquarters often to visit the widow and to engage in horseback rides, she on her gray pony and him on the beautiful Andalusian stallion she had offered to sell him many times, and which he might one day purchase. Her brother lived there with her and seemed to be in his right mind, but preferred solitude and seldom had anything to say.

Often, since the road to Estrella Duncan's home went near the Anderson ranch, he stopped in to share a cup of coffee and conversation with them. Twice on his short visits Sarah's son and the Indian woman Alta were there with the baby boy they called Quanah.

And they sometimes went for a walk into the pasture out back of the house to watch the new colt that had been born to Hub's mare on a cold day in October. The colt was a dun like his father, with ebony hoofs and a black mane and tail. And when he chased his mother across the open fields, that black tail hung in the wind behind him like a flag, sweeping the tops of the tall, golden grasses.

THE END